D0458272

Honeybees
and
Frenemies

Also by Kristi Wientge

Karma Khullar's Mustache

Honeybees
and
Frenemies

Kristi Wientge

Simon & Schuster Books for Young Readers

NEW YORK   LONDON   TORONTO   SYDNEY   NEW DELHI

To my Ohio family and friends,
who make coming home feel like I never left

ACKNOWLEDGMENTS

I am nothing on my own and this book would never have seen the light of day if it wasn't for the patient and relentless support of my agent, Patricia Nelson. Thank you, thank you.

Liz Kossnar pushed this story deeper and deeper until it became something I am proud of. Thank you for the e-mails and phone calls that got me through this. Lizzy Bromley, the cover of this book is what inspired me to complete it and do your art justice.

The Winged Pen has stood beside me despite my absence this year while my head was deep in revisions. A special shout-out to Julie, Gabrielle, Laurel, Rebecca, and Michelle for slogging through my first drafts and still offering to read for me! Mark Holtzen for timely and encouraging e-mails. Gabs and Michelle, you two have special stories and I'm glad you're a part of mine.

My family. Vinder for giving me wonderful material to work with. You were the character muse for Karma's dad and you were part of this story even before I realized it. My children who are my harshest critics and most enthusiastic supporters.

My parents deserve their very own paragraph because without their prayers I wouldn't be doing this.

My Ohio family, who makes visiting always feel like home. Nolan, Autumn, Brigand, and Adeza for dance offs, movie nights, and games. Nick and Pam, you're still Ohio family even if you're not always there. Big Papaw and Linda for loving and supporting us always. Aunt Beth, Uncle Mark, and gang for always welcoming my kids in like they're your own. Uncle John and Aunt Robin for giving us cars whenever we need one. Elizabeth Slamka for the late nights and Devoll Juniku for the good food. Brandy Slavens and family for keeping it real! Sara Hurt and your brood for lots of fun memories. Chris Shaw and family for long-distance friendships that pick up where they left off. Brooke McKasson, who is an honorary Ohioian friend because she's originally from the Midwest and is my partner in arson. We did set a tablecloth on fire in a nursing home.

My Heavenly Father, through whom all things are possible.

Chapter One

Random Bee Fact #37:
Honey is the only food that contains all the substances necessary to sustain life. That's why it's called the "Food of the Gods."

Once upon a time, this guy Newton said, "What goes up must come down."

I can't stand him.

I get it, gravity and all that. But there are other things that don't have gravity—like my feelings and life in general. So why does everything have to follow a stupid rule some guy discovered when an apple hit him on the head?

Maybe that apple gave him brain damage, because let's be honest, all he did was state the obvious. If he was really all that smart he would have been able to figure out how to keep things up and not let them come crashing down on his head. Or better, predict when things would fall in the first place.

No one ever warns you about stuff like that. It just comes out of nowhere, like bird poop right into your ice-cream cone. Sorry, that happened to me a few days ago and I'm still grossed out. That bird never shouted, "Bombs away!" and that apple never said to Newton, "Watch out!" In my case, what my best friend, Brooke, had just said was the apple . . . or the bird poop. I couldn't quite figure out which one.

Brooke sat across from me in our corner booth at Aunt Bee's Café. Between us was a yellow vase with a fake sunflower and even faker googly-eyed bee that stared too intensely at me. Brooke's eyes were all wide and practically exploding with stars, in a less creepy way than the fake bee, but they still made me rub nervously at my arms.

I couldn't get my mouth to work and say what I knew Brooke was waiting for me to say. Something along the lines of "Oh my gosh! I'm so happy for you! You've wanted to go to that band camp forever, and you got in!"

The green leather of the booth stuck to the backs of my legs, holding me in place even though I was desperate to move. Actually, desperate to do *anything* since I was still trying to convince myself that what she said was the complete opposite of what I heard. That she got it all wrong. That I misunderstood her.

It's not that I wasn't happy for her. I was. But this summer was supposed to be . . . well, different. Not the my-best-friend-is-gone-to-another-state-until-two-weeks-before-school-starts different. It wasn't as if I had the entire summer planned out on a calendar like Mom made us do at home, but it was the first summer Brooke and I were allowed to get dropped off places by ourselves. The pool, the strip mall (with the craft store, the bookstore, and the lotion place all in a row), the movies, the amusement park. We'd both gotten memberships to King's Island for Christmas and now Brooke's grandma would get her pass instead!

The honey straw in my hand dripped onto one of my crocheted wristbands. I sucked on it quickly before the honey could harden.

Brooke rubbed her finger up and down her glass of honey lemonade, tracing a drip that striped the side of her glass. "Camp's near the university by my aunt Pam's. Mom wants to make a big trip of it. We're leaving tomorrow," she said.

"What about King's Island? I can't go with your *grandma*." I yanked the wristband out of my mouth. I hated that that was the first thing I said. "That's not what

I meant to say. It's really cool you got into camp. It's just . . . It'll be so boring without you here."

Brooke nodded and tapped her fingers on her straw. She practiced the flute even without a flute in her hands. I was so used to it, I usually hardly noticed. What if she stopped doing that by the time I saw her again? Maybe one of those fancy music kids would tease her, or worse, she'd decide it was stupid and babyish.

These things could happen. It happened to Fran, my older sister, the summer before middle school. She went from my older sister who played Polly Pocket with me and spent hours outside on the trampoline, launching me until I could almost clear the top of the safety netting that lined it, to this total stranger who acted like I had a horrible disease and couldn't be seen in public with her.

"Stop staring at me like that, Flor. You're freaking me out."

"Sorry. I just want to remember you like this."

"Like what? It's just the summer, not the rest of our lives."

"I know," I mumbled, sucking up the rest of the honey in my straw, but closed my eyes and tried to remember exactly what she looked like. I opened my eyes, glad to see that I got each of her freckles exactly right. Five tiny ones on her left cheek, seven on her right, and the bigger one that sat right at the bridge of her nose, and her curly but never frizzy dark hair. "Here." I passed her the wristband that didn't have a slobber stain. I'd been working on the pattern for a few weeks. My favorite to make were thicker than normal bracelets and stretched over your hand so I didn't have to create any kind of clasp. I loved how they looked with the thin leather bracelets on my arm. "Wear this and I'll send you another one once I make a few more."

Brooke reached across the table for the wristband and admired it as she slipped it over her hand. I'd done a new crochet stitch pattern and used a silver yarn that had skinny threads of sparkly silver mixed in.

All of a sudden, the smell of vanilla perfume scratched my throat like I'd swallowed an itchy sweater. Candice Holloway leaned across our table. Uninvited.

"Did you hear?" she asked. She looked right at Brooke, then tossed her hair over her shoulder and barely let her eyes fall on me.

The way she stood, I could see right up her nose.

"Did we hear what?" Brooke asked, her eyes on me, giving her head a shake. Neither of us really cared what Candice had to say.

"The Honey Festival. They're having a sort of 'all-star' year. You know, for the fiftieth anniversary." Candice ran her hand under her hair and twisted it in front of her shoulder. "It's not really fair, if you ask me. All those poor third graders don't get a chance to participate this year. They have to wait and do a special pageant for the Apple Festival in the fall." She cocked her head to the side and blinked at me. Not in that fluttery way she did when she laughed too loud at Ryan Carter's jokes. It was definitely more of a fake innocent flutter.

Brooke put her crumpled-up napkin on top of her plate. "Let's go, Flor."

"Wait a minute, what do you mean 'all-star'?" The backs of my legs got even stickier and more stuck than a few minutes before. Those four honey straws were doing weird things in my stomach.

Candice slapped the *Western Star* newspaper onto the table. The front page read: "A Hive of Activity as Honeydale, Ohio, Reveals All-Star Reunion for 50th Honey Festival."

"The winners from the past ten years are competing for the crown." Candice waved her hand in the air like she wasn't the least bit freaked out. Why would she be? Our town lived for the Sauerkraut Fest in the spring, Honey Festival in the summer, the Apple Festival in fall, and the Christmas Parade in the winter. The Honey Festival was usually the only one that had any sort of pageant connected to it—if you could call a bunch of eight- and nine-year-olds waving from cars and doing cheesy dances a pageant.

I shook my head, mostly trying to get everything around me to stay still. Just like I was sure I'd misunderstood Brooke when she said she was going away all summer, I was sure the words in the newspaper must be wrong too.

"I heard the first Queen Bee is even coming back to town," Candice said with a sniff.

"Well, good luck," I managed to choke out.

"What do you mean?" Candice asked. "You have to be in it. Everyone who's ever won *has* to."

This could not be happening.

She looked at me like she still knew me and we hadn't been enemies for the past three years. "You're *afraid*. You don't think you can win," Candice said.

Of all people, she knew exactly why I hated the Honey Festival. She had ruined my life since third grade after I was crowned Little Miss Honeybee and she got first runner-up.

Brooke grabbed my arm. "Come on. Let's go."

I latched on to her arm, our wristbands lining up next to each other like one of those friendship charms that look broken when apart, but really they're just each other's missing pieces.

The moral of Newton's story was: Watch out for falling apples. Or in my case, run for cover. It would've been nice to have some sort of warning that I'd be losing my best friend to band camp and stuck spending the summer avoiding my enemy.

Chapter Two

Random Bee Fact #82:
It takes between 500 to 1,100 bee stings to be fatal to an
adult without a bee allergy.

A perfectly blue sky stretched out above me. Not a single inch gave any hint of the horrible fog of bad news that had decided to settle around me. Even the thought of having to somehow be part of the pageant hung in the air like the smell of a batch of my older sister Fran's kale chips sprinkled with nutritional yeast.

If this were a movie, the blue sky would mean Brooke and I were running around King's Island ready to sneak in a ride on the Drop Zone. Maybe even talking our parents into letting us stay until the fireworks at ten o'clock.

Instead, that blue sky just reminded me that not only

was my summer turning out to be a disaster, but also that Fran got to enjoy the perfect sky at her lifeguard job. Not that sitting in a chair twirling a whistle around your finger and talking with your friends was actually work. Fran complained about the perils of her job—annoying kids who splashed, making it difficult to see, or kids who ran instead of walked, or the times when kids almost drowned—but I knew that as usual, she was just making her life sound way more exciting and important than it really was.

I shoved the door of Dad's store open, making the bells that dangled in front of it clatter and clang instead of gently jingle like they were supposed to.

"Flor, just in time," Dad said. Packing peanuts clung to his arm hair as he waved me over. "You're gonna love this."

Unless that box contained a famous flutist who would give Brooke private lessons all summer so she could stay here, I really didn't think I'd "love" what was inside.

Dad pulled a puffy blanket-looking thing out of the box.

"I know it doesn't look like much, but your mom asked me to come up with some promo ideas and I came across this online and had it overnighted here. You know what they say: Visibility is how you attract customers!" He held up the thing, which now, all the way out of the box, looked more like an inflatable mattress you'd take camping. But puffier.

"Is it getting bigger?" I asked.

"They also say: Go big or go home!" He waited for me to laugh, but when I didn't he shrugged. "It was air-sealed in that plastic. Just taking shape. It's a mattress costume!" Dad did a big *ta-da* motion with his arms.

I stood there. Mouth opened. No words.

"Go on, try it on. Just slip it over your clothes." He pushed me toward the mirrored panels that lined the wall behind the counter. One of the panels popped open like a secret door into the break room and bathroom (which I always have to clean even though they're not supposed to be for customers, but Dad still let people use them).

Dad helped pull my foot through the hole at the bottom when my shoe got stuck and Velcroed the back of the costume once I was squished into it. My arms stuck out of the sides, but only from my elbows. "Are you sure this is how it fits?" I asked, my voice flat and muffled inside the costume. There was no hole for my face, just mesh eyeholes that I could barely see out of. The eyeholes were disguised to look like the dented-in tufted bits of the mattress and were set below my actual eyes.

"You've got sales in your blood, but it's a partnership. You bring 'em in, I do the sellin'."

I squeezed through the break room door and looked at myself in the mirrors. The mattress looked more like a giant bar of soap.

"Maybe a few springs coming out of the top like hair will make me look more like a mattress," I said.

"No, no. It'll look like we sell faulty mattresses. It's all about foam now, Flor. Multicomplex foam. Memory foam."

He started to do that thing with his hands like he was talking to a large crowd of people who deeply cared about mattresses.

"It's okay. I'll just be out here." I shoved through the door and onto the sidewalk to avoid listening to Dad's infomercial lecture about the newest mattress technology.

"Atta girl, Flor. Visibility equals . . ." Dad cocked his head, waiting for me to answer.

"Sales," I said, glad he couldn't see my face.

He nodded and then took a few fake golf swings with his invisible club.

I waddled up and down the sidewalk in front of the store, trying to get used to walking in the costume.

The tourist train blew its whistle as it slowly chugged into the station at the bottom of the hill. A few minutes later about twenty antiques lovers bustled up the sidewalk with their phones out, snapping pictures of me.

"Oh, looky at that bar of soap," a lady with red sunglasses said.

"That's a sponge."

"Where's the car wash?" the man next to the red sunglasses lady asked. "I told you we should have driven here. Save me from having to wash the car myself."

"If you brought the car, we couldn't have taken the train."

The funny thing was, the train chugged along at thirty miles per hour and only went between Honeydale and the next town over. They could have driven here faster, but Dad said it's all about the nostalgia, not the convenience.

The tourists wandered farther up the street, clamoring in and out of shops and the so-called museum, which was really a bunch of rooms filled with yellowing mannequins in dusty old clothes pretending to churn butter.

The mesh near my face was wet with the heat of my breath. How many minutes could you be in a mattress costume before suffocating to death?

A patter of feet and Mom's voice came from behind me.

"Excuse me. What are you doing?"

I turned around. The eyeholes only let me see the middle of her body, the worn-out flannel she always wore to teach art class thrown over a red tank top and the tiny flecks of paint splattered up and down her arms. I expected Mom to know it was me. I forgot she couldn't see my face. "Mom!"

"Wait. Florence? Is that you?" She leaned in closer. "What are you?" she asked in a half whisper.

"Yes, it's me," I yelled, not sure if I sounded as muffled to everyone else as I did to myself.

The plastic flapping sound of the OPEN-CLOSED sign hitting glass let me know Dad had come out of the store. "Mina! Great promo, huh?"

"This was your idea?" Mom's voice got squeakier and louder with each word.

I clenched my jaw tight, hoping this didn't turn into an all-out fight in the middle of the sidewalk. They'd been arguing a lot over the past few months, but here? Now? While I was trapped inside a mattress costume?

Dad reached toward Mom, putting his arm around her. "Aw, come on. Let's go inside and talk about it."

Mom sighed and followed Dad through the door. I stood outside like, well, like a mattress someone threw out by the road. Maybe if I stood there long enough a garbage truck would come pick me up. I might even wave one down and jump in the back myself.

Even that sounded like a better way to spend my summer than worrying about some stupid All-Star Festival and dealing with the ups and downs of Mom and Dad's fighting. All without Brooke.

Chapter Three

Random Bee Fact #16:
Worker bees don't get a say in anything. The scouts boss them around and tell them what they can and cannot do.

M om and Dad were still arguing about the mattress costume when I pushed through the door what felt like hours later, but was really only twenty minutes according to the clock behind the counter. I'd stood outside watching them, waiting for the fight to die down, but I guess because the entire storefront was glass they had to make themselves look like they were just working, not fighting.

"Flor, take that thing off and help me dust these bookshelves, please," Mom said.

Dad followed me into the break room and helped me out of the costume.

"Thanks, kid. We'll give you balloons next time. Visibility *and* freebies. Never underestimate the power of a free gift." Dad shoved the costume into a cubby beside the coffee maker and went back out front. I grabbed a few rags and the lemon dusting spray and followed.

"Mrs. Thorton," Mom said, her regular, not-fighting voice returning as the jingle of bells announced someone entering the store.

I fumbled with the dusting spray because my hands felt like I'd just eaten one of Fran's raw energy bars that coated my fingers in coconut oil at the sound of Mrs. Thorton's name.

Her eyes landed right on me before I could slip back into the break room. Mrs. Thorton owned Thorton's Mulch and Landscaping, and whenever there was a city council election, her face was plastered on those signs you stick in your yard. She was my gram's good friend. Mrs. Thorton also happened to be in charge of the Honey Festival.

"Hi, Mina. Kingsley." She nodded at Mom and Dad, but her gaze was locked in on me. "Florence." Her voice had a singsong-ness to it.

I cleared my throat. The lemon smell of the dusting

spray stung my eyes and coated my mouth. I might be the only person in Honeydale who didn't share Candice's and Mrs. Thorton's love of the festival.

"I'm sure you all know why I'm here." She held up a folder. "I've got the festival schedule and paperwork I need signed." She tore her eyes off of me and turned to Mom and Dad. "It's going to be big this year."

"Oh, Flor, isn't it exciting?" Mom didn't even look back as me before she rushed toward Mrs. Thorton to look at the paperwork.

Mrs. Thorton looked around the store. "This could mean big business for our town, Kingsley. Don't you think? Just imagine the crowds."

Dad nodded. "I guess it couldn't hurt." He turned to me and said, "That costume and those crowds." Dad shook his head like he could see sales go up. "That's a win-win."

"Flor, put those things down and let's go in the break room and talk this over," Mom said, ushering Mrs. Thorton behind the counter and into the break room.

"Tea, Sally?"

"Yes, please," Mrs. Thorton said, placing the files on the table.

Mom raised her eyebrows and bug-eyed me, pushing her chin toward the mugs. I clicked the switch on the electric kettle to get the hot water going for tea.

"Well, now," Mrs. Thorton said, settling into one of Gram's old dining chairs she left in here after Gramps died and she moved to Florida. "You really have grown, haven't you, Florence?" Then she turned to Mom. "A spitting image of you, Mina."

I sucked in my breath, glad I had the clatter of the mugs to cover up my sigh. Every time someone talked about my looks or mom's it always ended with them comparing me to some kind of food or drink. The way people in town described me made me feel like a specialty on display at the chocolate factory across from Dad's store. Almond eyes, caramel skin. It made me hungry.

"You've got the Valandingham build, though," Mrs. Thorton continued. "I remember when your father went through that same awkward gangly stage. Don't worry, dear, he grew out of it." She laughed so deep and chesty I expected her to break into a coughing fit, but she didn't. "I spoke to your grandma just this morning. Told her you'd be in the festival again. I still remember your grand-dad's reaction when they called your name. He cried and laughed and started hugging everyone around him."

Back in third grade Mrs. Thorton wasn't in charge of the pageant. She'd taken over a few years ago when she first became a city council member. I brushed some cracker crumbs off the counter as I waited for the water to boil, and let Mom take the conversation over from there. Mrs. Thorton even had a copy of the paper Mom signed for me from the summer before third grade. Mom showed it to me with a weird grin on her face. It all felt like I was playing the part of the innocent baby in Rumpelstiltskin: Mom had signed me up in third grade and now it was back to haunt me. Not only that, she was actually happy to sign me over to Mrs. Thorton-stiltskin and her evil festival schemes. Again.

I set the mugs on the table and sat down next to Mom, scanning each page Mrs. Thorton pushed across to her for any excuse to not be able to participate. I wished I had allergies to honey or a life-threatening reaction to large crowds of people, because looking at those papers only reminded me of Candice's betrayal after my winning in third grade.

Things were normal between us until school started and Candice told some girls in our class that I only won because my parents threatened to sue the town for discrimination if I didn't. Another version of the rumor was that the town didn't have a choice because they had to choose someone of color.

It wasn't like I could defend myself or argue back. That'd have only made it seem true. Not that my parents would sue the town, but true that my skin was the reason I'd been chosen. And that had only been the beginning of the end of our friendship.

I used to enjoy the festival. It was the highlight of summer even if it meant summer was over. The Honey Festival was one long day of eating everything, running around blocked-off streets, getting sticky with sweat and honey, watching the parade filled with fancy cars, and the pageant with the frilly dresses and waiting to see who'd get the crown.

It was still fun. As long as I didn't have to be a part of it.

Mrs. Thorton flipped the manual to the calendar of events leading up to the festival.

I thought Mom's family calendar was freakily organized and color-coded, but this festival calendar was worse. Only Sundays were blank. My entire summer was going to be mapped out for me in green, pink, yellow, and blue.

Mom stood up to grab the sugar while Mrs. Thorton explained about the festival rules. "As you can see, we have a full summer ahead. In light of it being the fiftieth anniversary, we've come up with the theme 'Bee Aware.' This year we're focusing more on raising awareness of bees dying and what we can do to save them. Whoever is crowned queen this year will continue on as a bee ambassador, traveling to other festivals and spreading bee knowledge."

This whole thing had gotten way more serious. In third grade all we had to do was write two hundred and fifty words about bees. I entered a poem called "Fuzzy Buzzy Bee" about a bee that was so extra fuzzy, he was like a super pollen collector.

Mrs. Thorton stacked some stray papers as she continued to talk. "I'm contacting all the queens from the past ten years. If the queens aren't available, I'm asking the first runners-up, but it's good to know I can depend on you, Florence."

This was my chance. I didn't actually have to do this. "Actually, Mrs. Thorton," I said as she pulled out a few more papers, "I'd rather let Candice take the spot."

I was only giving Candice what she wanted because it was exactly what I didn't want.

"Florence," Mom said, her mouth hanging open the way she always told me not to. "This isn't the kind of thing you say no to. It's a commitment and you should follow through."

Mrs. Thorton put her hand up. "It's okay, Mina. I can ask Candice. I mean, of course, I had hoped you would participate, but I'll just give her a call." Mrs. Thorton pulled out her phone and started to dial. "I was just at the café. I wish I'd known; I would have told Candice right then. She was practically begging me. Something about finally taking the honeybee part of our festival more seriously. She'd be perfect for the ambassador position if she won." Mrs. Thorton tapped her fingers on the table. "Yes, hello. Hi, Patty. I'm just at Kingsley's store, and Florence doesn't want to participate. Candice is in."

Pause.

It gave me a minute to think about what was happening. I didn't mind giving Candice what she wanted as long as it meant I also got what I wanted—out of the festival. But this didn't feel like a "win-win" deal like Dad talks about. Candice thought I was afraid. She thought I couldn't win. Giving her my spot felt like I was proving her right.

"I knew she'd be so happy. Of course, she'll be—"

I hated the festival, but even more than that, I hated for Candice to think she was right. "I take it back!" I shouted. Then I lowered my voice and said, "Candice can't be in the festival. I want to."

"Just a minute, Patty. Yes, yes. Just hold on." Mrs. Thorton cupped her hand over her phone. "Florence, I just . . . Candice really has her heart set on this."

"But I changed my mind. I promise I'll do a good job." What was I doing? I'd had my way out and now I was begging to get back in.

Mrs. Thorton shook her head. "Yes, Patty. I'm here.

Yes, of course. Can I call you back?" She cleared her throat, giving me a frustrated look. "Sure, I'll walk over once I'm finished here. Bye."

"Florence." Mrs. Thorton set her phone loudly on the table. "I'm glad you want to participate, but changing your mind like that puts me in an awkward situation."

Not as awkward as my situation. "I'm sorry, Mrs. Thorton. I got to thinking, and I'd really like to be in the festival."

"Well, it's not like I can tell Candice she's out after I just told her mother she's in. This is ridiculous."

"Mrs. Thorton," Mom said, "I understand this is unprecedented, but if both girls are eager to participate, maybe we can work something out?"

Mrs. Thorton took a long sip of tea. "I suppose you girls could work together. Compete as one contestant. Hmm." She took another sip of tea, her eyes watching me over the top of the mug. She set the mug down and put her hands, still hot from the tea, on mine. "I think that's a great idea. You and Candice. Working together."

I pulled my hands out from hers slowly, smiling and nodding to cover up the nervousness that skittered through my body. "Thank you, Mrs. Thorton."

"Never mind." She waved her hands in the air. "We have a lot to get through. These are the events. Lunch at the nursing home, craft hour at the library, and the Multiple Sclerosis Ball just before the festival are the bigger events. All contestants are required to attend." She pushed a clipboard in front of me. "As you can see, volunteering is also a requirement. There are lots of options. Picking up litter in the park, reading books at the nursing home." She pointed at each one with the end of her pen. "But, since you're now working with Candice, I think I have the perfect job for you two. A member of our community needs some help with his yard work. It's quite a task." She turned to Mom. "You know Mr. Henry. He fell cleaning his gutters and is in a wheelchair for a few weeks."

"Mr. Henry?" Mom asked with a frown. Mrs. Thorton exchanged a look with Mom that weighed so heavily with meaning that if it were a cloud, it'd have poured rain all over the table and probably struck me with lightning.

"Who's Mr. Henry?" I asked.

Mrs. Thorton waved her hand at my question like she could erase my words right out of the air. "Besides, Mina, the girls will be working together."

Mom and Mrs. Thorton turned and smiled expectantly at me. The way they'd just shared that look, turning at almost the exact same time, wearing those matching smiles, thinking Candice and I would work well together—all sure signs I'd been transported to a parallel universe. On the flip side, there was another me at King's Island with Brooke. I opened my mouth hoping an excuse would pop into my head and explode out.

"Actually, I've promised Fran I'd help out at the food pantry. You know, she's been *so* busy since she took over for my grandma." A drop of guilt, slow and sticky like honey from a honey straw, dripped off my words. I really shouldn't have told a lie using Gram and her beloved food pantry.

"Oh, I didn't know you were already volunteering this summer." Mrs. Thorton nodded her head approvingly and scribbled something down on her notepad. "Candice can help you and Fran with the food pantry as well so you aren't so overwhelmed with your duties. This is exactly what we're looking for. Teamwork and a sense of community. Great qualities in a future Queen Bee. We all can learn a lot from your willingness." Mrs. Thorton smacked her hands down on the table. She grabbed a napkin and dabbed her shiny face. "That just about covers it, except for one last thing. Everyone will need to get their talents approved in two weeks. You and Candice will have to decide what you'll perform together. We want this to be B-I-G, big. Well, I better get going, I just need you to sign here that you received the information."

I slumped farther down into the chair; the wood part

in the middle digging into my spine, sending jolts of anger through me. It was my own stupid lie that had so happily and quickly pushed Candice even more into my life.

The pen moved so slowly, each letter too sharp and angled without any squiggles. Signing your death warrant didn't really inspire a flourish.

Chapter Four

Random Bee Fact #25:
Trained bees are better at identifying smells than dogs.

Talent.

Approval.

Two weeks.

Not only was my third-grade attempt at a talent laughable, it was also the main thing Candice had teased me about after I'd been crowned Little Miss Honeybee. Now we had to come up with a talent we could perform together.

In third grade the festival was a parade where we rode through town driving at about three miles per hour and then standing around onstage and wishing we were with our families sucking on honey-flavored ice cream instead of wearing sweaty, itchy dresses.

Our moms told us what to do for the talent. I did a Bollywood dance that was pretty much me spinning in a circle and pumping my arms up and down in the air to about thirty seconds of a Bollywood song. I loved Bollywood back then. I think it was the colors and the music, especially when the actors cried and got all dramatic.

After I won, Candice joined in when a few of the other girls whispered when I walked by at school the next day. She made fun of me in that quiet way, smiling without laughing at the jokes and listening to the teasing without saying anything. It was like she forgot *she* watched Bollywood and lined her arms with every bangle Fran and I had while jingling around my living room dancing right along with me.

I hated everything about that pageant. Because the day I won was the day Candice went from being my best friend to my worst enemy.

Those memories made the blueberry goat's-milk yogurt in front of me taste even more like sour baby spit. I glared at Fran as she finished off the last banana. It was her fault our fridge was stuffed full of cashew cheeses and almond water—I refused to pretend it was milk.

Fran caught me glaring and scrunched her face in that annoying way she saved just for me.

"I've got a lot of jobs for you and Candice when you come to the food pantry on Friday."

"Mom," I groaned.

Mom cleared her throat and tapped her finger on the family calendar that hung from the side of the fridge when Dad walked into the kitchen. "Things are going to start getting busy. Be sure you stick your Post-its on the calendar before our family meeting next week." Mom had a way of saying things to everyone while simultaneously managing to shine a glaring interrogation light on a single person. Usually me. Lately Dad. Or a combination of us both.

Dad nodded to let Mom see he'd heard her, then stuck his head in the fridge, scanning the shelves of the refrigerator for something non-Fran-sprouted or soaked. Probably wishing a doughnut would appear like I had. I'd learned to lower my standards this past year since Fran started taking her "affordable healthy eating" seriously. When Gram moved to Florida, Fran took over the church's food pantry for her and we'd been eating her experiments ever since.

Gram had always made casseroles for the families to eat when they came in each week to collect their canned goods. She'd share the recipes with them and be sure they took home enough cans to make a few of the recipes. Fran took it a step further and tried to create new recipes that could be made with only canned goods, since some of Gram's recipes still needed meat and cheese from the grocery store.

"We'd better get going, Flor," Mom said. "I hope everyone's taken note of the schedule for this week." She twisted the cap on her travel mug, pushing a whiff of her dandelion root drink replacement for coffee right up my nose. As if the smell of real coffee wasn't bad enough—like a perfume with a bitter after-smell that was nice just before burning your nose hairs. "I told Mrs. Holloway we'd pick Candice up outside the café."

Mom drove toward town and Aunt Bee's Café in a wooly blanket of silence, making me squirmy and uncomfortable. She and Dad had been fighting so much, giving her one less reason to get annoyed was something small I could do. Even if it meant spending a few hours a week with Candice.

"I know Candice isn't your favorite person," Mom said, her eyes flickering to me in the rearview mirror.

Part of me was surprised Mom actually noticed. She knew Candice had said some mean things, but she didn't know everything Candice had done.

"Third grade was a long time ago. I think it'll be good if you spend the summer building bridges instead of sulking."

I glared at the back of Mom's head.

She kept her eyes glued to the mostly empty road.

"I can't build bridges, I'll be busy doing yard work."

"Very funny." Mom forced a smile across her face and said good morning to Candice when she climbed into the backseat.

Candice's smile was more squinty eyes than mouth smile. I smiled back, making sure no teeth peeked out. Mom pulled back onto the road and Candice and I took turns snatching glances at each other, the way you grab cards while playing Spoons—watchful and suspicious.

I was also waiting for Candice to say something about how I'd messed up her plans to rule the festival.

"You looking forward to the festival, Candice?" Mom asked.

"Oh, yes. I'm really looking forward to working with Florence and helping around the community." Candice somehow managed to simultaneously talk, smile, and be polite—basically a parent's dream—all in one short sentence while also sneaking a warning glare in my direction—basically my nightmare.

Mom might force me to build a bridge, but no one said I had to cross it. Especially if all that was waiting for me on the other side was exactly what I'd been avoiding for three years—spending time with Candice.

I glared out the car window until Mom turned onto a gravel road I didn't even know existed—and I'd lived in Honeydale my entire life. "Where're we going?"

"Mr. Henry lives off this gravel road," Mom said.

The gravel road was squished between trees so heavy with leaves and twisted with thick branches that I couldn't see anything except the road in front of us. Suddenly the thick line of trees disappeared, revealing a huge white farmhouse with a green metal roof that sat at the top of a hill. It was the White House. Not the one in Washington, DC. But the one that no kid in all of Honeydale, Ohio, dared talk about except in hushed whispers.

Candice slapped her hand over her mouth. I tried to swallow, but the sour goat yogurt from breakfast decided to return, burning the back of my throat in a way that I was afraid if I swallowed I'd be sick.

"Mom! You mean Mr. Henry is the Old Man on the Hill?" I didn't even know that guy had an actual name. Suddenly that look Mom and Mrs. Thorton shared right over my head and the way Mrs. Thorton offered for Candice to help me all connected like the final loop of a complicated crochet stitch. "You can't just leave us here alone. Haven't you heard the stories? Kids at school say he keeps the Girl Scouts who've climbed up his driveway in the freezer next to the boxes of their very own cookies."

Look, it's not like I *really* believed it, but still. Something about that house so far up the hill screamed: Leave me alone or you'll never be seen again!

"Florence, that is complete nonsense. He's just . . . a little odd and grumpy," Mom said.

"And creepy," I muttered.

Candice squeezed and pulled at her bottom lip—a habit of hers I shouldn't still remember. Somehow it made me feel better knowing she also didn't know who Mr. Henry was before then and was just as freaked out as I was.

Mr. Henry's driveway was the longest I'd ever been on. It went on as long as the central stretch of Main Street.

When we reached the top, the driveway wove around the big white house. At the back of the house, hidden from the road, there was a massive garage. Mom, slower than slow, backed her car in front of the first of five garage doors. *Five.* Not even Gramps had had that many cars even when he was at the peak of restoring old ones.

"Whoa, he must be the richest person in Honeydale," I said.

"He used to own that big building behind the soccer fields, Henry Corporation," Mom said, opening her door and stepping out of the car.

I continued to take in everything around us. From the road, the house looked smallish. I wondered how many people had been up here. The hill flattened out at one side of the big white house, extending to a huge barn. Cattails stuck up out of the ground behind the barn where a pond must be.

"Girls, wait here while I go speak to Mr. Henry," Mom said.

Candice and I stood by Mom's car while she made her way to the big green door with empty flowerpots on either side.

A breeze pushed my hair across my face. I turned toward the wind to let it brush my hair out of my mouth, and then stopped. The hill was like the Eiffel Tower replica at King's Island; it didn't seem very high until you stood at the top and looked down. Tiny cars crawled along the four-lane road below, no bigger than my pinkie fingernail. Beyond that I could see the part of Main Street with some fast-food restaurants and, just beyond that, the historic district. The buildings were small, but I could make out things like the church steeple, the orange tin roof of the antiques store, the copper roof of the library that was more green than rust-colored.

"Whoa." Candice's mouth hung wide open.

I turned to watch her look at the town. It was weird seeing someone the complete opposite of you react to things the same way as you. Part of me forgot Candice was still an actual human being and not just a robot who'd had her system rewired to "mean mode" one day.

She turned and caught me watching her and we both snapped out of our daze. I pulled at the green crocheted choker around my neck, pretending I'd only just looked her way. Maybe I needed to loosen the choker; it was suddenly too tight.

"It smells gross up here," Candice said, her face turning from smooth and calm to squished and annoyed in a single second.

I dipped my head to sniff at my armpits, trying to think back to morning and if I'd remembered to put on deodorant, even though I think she was talking about the soured grass smell that lingered and not BO.

"Smells fine to me," I said, and turned back toward the house. "If it's so smelly, you could just tell Mrs. Thorton you have another volunteering job to do. There was a whole list of other stuff." I didn't want Candice thinking it'd been my idea to work with her.

"Or maybe you could drop out. Again."

I turned to say something back, but Mom was walking toward the car.

"He's not answering the door." Her keys jangled together with each step. "Mrs. Thorton said she'd left him messages. I'll get in touch with him later and set it up for us to come by later in the week."

Candice sighed and flung the car door open. She probably

thought this was all my fault too. I wondered what she'd rather be doing. Third-grade Candice and I made bracelets out of yarn scraps and drew comics, but something about Candice's silver bracelets, dangly earrings, and shoes that every other girl in our grade had been wearing this year told me she wasn't into homemade anymore.

"It's a shame," Mom said, her hand on the car door but not making any effort to open it. "If we don't tackle some of these flower beds soon, they'll be bare all summer. Not to mention all these leaves and branches. You can't even see the grass."

I pulled my door open and as I slid into the backseat, the air near the barn blurred like a mirage. I blinked my eyes and shook my head, not quite understanding what I was seeing.

Mom raised her hand over her eyes and squinted in the same direction. "What are you looking at?"

I jog-walked around the front of the car toward the barn. Maybe that was the way mirages worked, made your feet move toward it even though your brain was telling you to stay put.

As I got closer, I still couldn't quite make sense of what was in front of me.

A man-shaped statue was covered in moving, buzzing bees.

The grass crunched behind me as Mom and Candice breathed heavily beside me.

"Is that Mr. Henry?" Candice asked.

"It's a scarecrow, isn't it?" It hadn't even crossed my mind that it could be a real-life human under all those bees.

"What's he trying to do? He could get killed." For once Mom, Queen of Preparedness, didn't have a plan on how to handle something like this.

"It's okay," Candice said, putting a hand on Mom's arm. "Dad once had a man come to the orchard and do something like this. He could get the bees to make all kinds of shapes and patterns on his body."

"Mr. Henry?" Mom called in a not-too-loud voice.

Maybe it was just me, but I swear the buzzing got louder. Like the bees were answering Mom. I rubbed my arms as we waited to see what would happen. Candice dodged a stray bee and moved closer to Mom.

There was movement, like Mr. Henry had lifted his arms. The bees moved along, rising in a cluster as he took something from around his neck and placed it in a cardboard box at his feet. Then, his entire body rose onto his good foot since the other one stuck out straight like it was in a cast. He leaned forward. I rushed in front of him without thinking, Candice only one step behind me, but before we could reach him, he hopped and all the bees fell from his body in a thick, fuzzy blanket that kept a hint of his body's shape before going in all directions.

The bees swarmed around the box, like they were searching for something. Only a few bees hovered near Mr. Henry, now clearly sitting in a wheelchair, somehow looking even scarier than I'd imagined from all the stories I'd heard.

Chapter Five

Random Bee Fact #78:
Fifteen billion dollars' worth of fruits, nuts, and
vegetables are pollinated by bees annually.

I swear the air itself hummed and spread through my body like a rumble of thunder, first in my chest, then all the way down to my feet and the tips of my fingers. The whole thing had been almost magical. Weird, but magical.

Mom cleared her throat. "Impressive. I don't think I've ever seen anything like that."

Mr. Henry nodded and started to wheel past us toward his house.

His hair was fine and white. The skin under his eyes puffed in a saggy kind of way. His shoulders were broad and he looked too big and strong for the wheelchair, like when Brooke's younger brothers squished into her old doll strollers.

"Before you go," Mom said, blocking Mr. Henry from going around us, "it's just . . . I believe Mrs. Thorton has been trying to contact you. I brought the girls here. . . . It's for volunteering. The Honey Festival committee. We heard you'd been injured and might need help with some yard work."

I'd never heard Mom speak in half sentences.

"Yes, sir. On behalf of the Honey Festival, we're here to help," Candice said, stepping forward. I half expected her to put her hands on her hips and have a yellow-and-black-striped cape billow out from behind her. "I'm Candice Holloway." Her voice shook, and I watched her throat as she swallowed. Maybe her superhero speech was more of a mask rather than a billowy cape.

"Holloway. I know that name. Aunt Bee's Café." Mr. Henry grunted and pushed the wheels of his chair forward.

I lunged toward Mr. Henry to help him push his chair. Candice might have been the first to introduce herself, but I'd be the first to help out.

Mr. Henry swatted at my hands. "I don't need your help gettin' around."

Mom put her hand on my arm. "Mr. Henry, the girls

mean no harm. They're just hoping to extend a helping hand on behalf of the community." Mom pulled me next to her. "This is my daughter, Florence Amrita Valandingham."

Mr. Henry raised his eyebrows in recognition of my last name. Like most people in Honeydale, he must have known my grandpa. Having a shop downtown meant most of the town at least knew your face. Having a last name like Valandingham meant people knew my grandpa and my dad and most likely my sister, and all those expectations got lumped right onto me. Usually people didn't know just by looking at me. Carrying the Valandingham name but none of the looks made people do a double take. Fran was a spitting image of Gram and Dad, with green eyes and sandy brown hair. I was the only one who took after Mom—dark hair and big brown eyes.

"Well, that name is bigger than her and then some." He wheeled himself forward, and looked me up and down. "Like a beanpole."

"Thank you, sir." I didn't even know why I said that, it just came out.

"Is it free?" Mr. Henry asked.

"Excuse me?" asked Mom.

"You don't want any donation, do you?"

"Oh, no, sir," Candice said.

"Hmm. Yard work, you say?" He pushed past us

toward a makeshift ramp of plywood over the steps that led to the front door. "You'll find the rakes and things in the barn. Don't make too much noise, and I hope you brought your own water."

"Of course," Mom said, but he'd already closed the door. "All right, girls. You heard the man. Just start by raking this place so we can at least see the grass. I'll be back in an hour and I'll bring some sandwiches and see if we can't soften him up. No one ever says no to my ham salad."

That wasn't true. Fran always said no to ham salad.

"We'll be sure to have as much done as we can, Mrs. V." Candice's words were like raisins covered in chocolate—sweet on the outside, but under that a wrinkled, sour truth. I knew she wasn't as sweet as she pretended to be.

"I'll get the rakes," I said, and walked toward the barn before I accidentally said something mean out loud. At least when I said something, it was what and how I meant.

When I got to the back corner of the barn, I took a deep breath and prepared myself to start pulling up the jungle of weeds that were as thick and tall as small trees and deal with candy-coated Candice for an hour. As the air hit the back of my throat it tasted like the smell of our dumpster by the end of the week—when I'd hold my breath and throw the garbage bag in and run away before the lid could slam closed.

I coughed out the air and held my breath as I peeked around the side of the barn. I did it slowly, fully aware that I was at the Old Man on the Hill's house. The very old man who, it was rumored, built the house so high up so he could get rid of the bodies of his victims before the cops reached the top of his driveway.

Before I could convince myself the smell wasn't that of dead bodies, a crinkle of plastic and the shuffle of feet came from behind me. I lifted up the rake and opened my mouth to scream as I turned around.

"Flor, what are you doing?" Candice stood there. Those blackish-green garbage bags in either hand, staring at me like I forgot to put on a pair of shorts when I left the house.

I glanced around Candice toward the house, looking for any kind of curtain ruffle or silhouette near a window, but the whole house sat under the shadows of a few large trees.

"Candice, there's a weird smell back here and I just wanted to see if . . . you know?"

Candice shook her head. "No, I don't know."

"What if it's true? My mom might have left us up here with a murderer."

"You don't actually believe any of that, do you?"

"Okay, if you don't believe any of it, then you go check."

Candice scrunched the empty garbage bags under one arm and reached for the rake. "I'm telling you, there's not going to be anything there."

I pulled the rake closer to me. "Then why do you want the rake?"

"It could be a dead animal or something." Her voice was sure, but her eyes flicked to either side of me.

"I'm keeping the rake—you don't even think anything's there." I squeezed my fingers around its handle and stepped around the back of the barn, right behind Candice.

A yellowed deep freezer and a black refrigerator sat in the grass. Only a few scraggly weeds crawled up their sides. Even the weeds were scared of what they'd find inside.

"Omigosh, omigosh, omigosh." I squeezed my eyes closed, dropped the rake, and clung to Candice like a cat to a tree.

"Shhhhhh," Candice hissed, looking back toward Mr. Henry's house. "What are we going to do?"

I fumbled to pick the rake up, holding the handle out in front of me, the tines digging into my ribs as I walked closer to the deep freezer. I paused in front of it and turned to Candice. "Get your phone out. We'll need pictures as evidence." I shoved the handle under the lip of the freezer cover and pushed down on the rake handle, prying the top open.

There wasn't a horror-movie creaking as it opened. There wasn't even a smell. "Hurry," I said, leaning to keep the lid pried open.

Candice held out her phone, but kept her head turned away as she took a few blind shots of the inside of the freezer.

"What in Sam Hill are you two doing?"

In a fraction of a second, I yanked the rake and pulled it behind my back, fully aware it stuck out way too obviously, as Candice slid her phone into her back pocket. Both of our faces froze in knowing we were caught and couldn't even think of a good enough explanation to dig our way out. How did you explain to someone you were expecting to find a rotting corpse in their abandoned deep freezer?

Mr. Henry rolled right in front of the black fridge, the wheels cracking sticks in half as he crept forward. The rake slipped from my hands and Candice's shoulders twitched with each snap of the twigs. I did my best to stand still, but couldn't stop from blinking at each and every sound.

"You shouldn't be back here."

"We were just looking for a place to pile the bags," Candice said.

"Yeah, once we had a few filled up," I added, snatching

the empty bags from under Candice's arm and holding them up. "Well, we better get busy." I grabbed Candice's arm and started to pull her back toward the driveway.

"It's not what you think," Mr. Henry said.

We both stopped. Frozen.

"I've heard the rumors. I'm old, but not deaf."

Candice squeezed her arms closer to her body. My hand was still around her arm so now it was trapped just under her armpit.

"If you want to know what that smell is, follow me."

The breaking of twigs was like dried bones as he pushed his wheelchair forward. The cracks and pops grew quieter and we realized he'd rolled away from us, not closer.

I let out a breath and Candice dropped her hands to her sides. I turned to go after him. Candice grabbed my arm. "Are you really going to follow him?" she asked.

It wasn't that I was suddenly so brave, more like I was sick of being scared and sick of being stuck—stuck doing things I didn't have a say in. "What else are we going to do? We can't hide here until my mom gets back." I picked up the rake and pointed at a shovel leaning against the barn. "Grab that. Between these and the two of us, we should be fine."

We crunched along behind Mr. Henry as he made his way toward the tree line just beyond the barn, the smell becoming more like rotten meat the closer we got. Under the canopy of shade and dampness the trees made, there were about five white rectangular boxes that were about as high as my waist sitting on cinder blocks. There wasn't anything special about them, they were just plain wooden boxes, but with dark black and brown char marks up the sides, and they were splintered and soggy-looking like no one had taken care of them in a long time.

"Dead bees," Candice said. Her voice was so whispery, it sounded like she actually felt sorry for the bees.

"It can't be bees. Smells more like a dead bear." I couldn't even breathe through my nose.

"Half my bees were hit with bacteria over the winter," Mr. Henry said. "Had to move the infected hives over here and burn the frames to keep it from spreading."

"I've read that mites have been quite bad this year too," Candice said.

"What are mites?" I asked, regretting it the second it was out of my mouth because Candice shook her head and sighed.

"They're little bugs that take over the hives and kill all the eggs and make the bees sick."

Of course Candice knew what mites were.

"I expect you girls to stay away from the back of the barn. And pile the wood separate. Real barn wood goes for a pretty penny these days." He wheeled back toward his house, leaving us with more questions than before he came.

Chapter Six

Random Bee Fact #11:
Bees have a brain the size of a grass seed, but can figure out complicated math problems faster than computers.

The bunk bed in the back corner of Dad's store was one of the only places I could hang out without being bothered. When I lay down on the top bunk, no one could see me unless, of course, they came into the store to buy a bunk bed. But considering how slow things had been lately, I was willing to take my chances.

I finished checking the store's e-mails and Web page. For my coding club project I'd set up an online shop for the store. The site was pretty simple and everything was linked to the e-mail account, but we'd gotten regular inquiries and sales. The messages were mostly spam, and

only one real question about the thickness of a brand of
mattress. I left that for Dad to answer later and climbed
onto the top bunk. (Which was no easy feat, considering
Dad had put those clear plexiglass panels over all the bunk
bed ladders to keep kids from climbing.) I stepped on the
headboard part of the bottom bunk and pulled the rest of
my body onto the top.

The "Don't sit" signs applied to me, too. There were
no perks to being the daughter of the guy who owned the
store. Seriously, I think the rules were actually meant for
me and no one else.

I squirmed toward the wall side of the top bunk with
Mom's phone and a skein of orange yarn I'd stashed in the
break room.

Mom wouldn't be back from her painting class for
another hour or so and Dad was in the break room having
his lunch. He'd only come out for a customer, so I had my
yarn and the top bunk all to myself.

Mom didn't like being distracted by technology when
she was in her "painting zone," so I had her phone. I tapped
in her passcode: 000000. She might as well not have one. I
scrolled to Brooke's name and typed:

How's camp?

You wouldn't believe what happened today!

My fingers hovered over the keypad as I thought about

how Candice and I had actually been up at the Old Man on the Hill's house, seen him covered in bees, opened the freezer behind his barn, stood next to him, and promised to go back on Thursday.

How was I supposed to explain to Brooke about Candice or Mr. Henry in a text? I deleted the second line and added:

Wish you were here. xoxo

I threw Mom's phone to the side and wrapped the bright orange yarn around two of my fingers, making a pretzel shape, and cast on my hook. Then I single crocheted, which basically looked like a braid, for about twenty stitches. I'd learned to crochet when I turned seven. Gramps spent a lot of time in bed between his treatments and Gram taught me as we sat next to him over the three years he was sick.

I decided to make the wristbands I'd promised Brooke, working in back stitch only because it's stretchy and perfect for pulling on and off. It was an easy pattern that let me kind of fuzz over my thoughts. I couldn't believe it'd only been a few days ago that Brooke and I'd been sitting at Aunt Bee's, when my summer turned inside out like a dirty sock, trapping me inside with nowhere else to go.

As I repeated the same stitches over and over, it was easy to not think of Candice and the festival and what in the world we'd do for our talent. Twenty single crochet back stitch only, turn, twenty half-double crochet back stitch only, turn, repeat, repeat, repeat.

I slipped one wristband on to see how it looked and started on the second when the bells over the front door banged together. The break room door slid open.

"I thought you were going to have the signs done for the sale." Mom's voice wasn't a yell, but it fizzed as if the words wanted to overflow loud and fast like a blender without a lid.

The flicker of a fight that'd started between Mom and Dad that morning at home sparked and practically exploded like a firework.

I pulled the yarn tight around my fingers and closed my eyes, wanting it to stop, but also wanting to hear it so I could understand why things had gone from normal to terrible over the past few months. When Gramps was alive and he and Dad ran the store together, the place always felt alive even when it was empty for days on end. I spent most days after school in the break room doing my homework until Gram or Mom would pick Fran and me up and take us home for dinner. There had never been talk about how to keeping the store going. It just kept going.

"It's a slow day," Dad said. The calm of how he spoke made Mom's voice sound angrier.

"What about the early bird catching the worm?" Mom asked, using one of Dad's sales mottos, but not in the go-get-'em way Dad said it. Mom made it sound more like we were the worms getting eaten instead of the birds getting their tasty reward.

"I took a longer lunch break, Mina. I'll get started on it now."

The computer chair squeaked and the wheels rolled across the tiles.

Things were quiet and I thought about climbing down and walking over to the front desk and telling Dad about the e-mail, even though that'd mean they'd find a job for me. But Mom spoke, stopping me at the top of the ladder.

"I called my parents again."

"Oh." Dad continued to clatter on the keyboard.

"They're willing to help out for three more months of rent, but honestly, I just don't know if that'll be enough. I think I should take the girls to New Jersey. Let them see my parents and the town. Maybe take a look at the school, some houses. Rethink that job offer I had."

"Not that again. We already decided. It's Fran's senior year. And now Florence has the festival." Dad sounded like Mom when she had to tell me twenty times to make my bed.

I knew Mom was annoyed Dad wasn't taking the slowness of the store more seriously, but I guess it never hit me exactly how serious things were. Not move-to-New-Jersey kind of serious. Plus, since Mom had her high school reunion and heard about an art teaching job at her old school last year, she brought it up every few weeks when she and Dad would fight.

"We don't need your parents' money." Dad's words splattered in that heavy way, like someone throwing a handful of wet sand onto the ground.

The chair squeaked again and the wheels slid across the tile, ending in a bang, probably hitting the wall behind the front desk. The bells crashed against the door so hard they clunked together without any sort of jingle. I stared out the big storefront windows, catching a flash of Dad walking up the sidewalk.

The computer keys clattered again and I slid down the side of the bunk bed.

Mom's head was down, staring at the computer screen.

I put her phone on the counter, letting it hit harder than I'd meant.

"Hey, Flor." Mom looked at me like she'd forgotten I existed.

I squinted at her, daring her to explain what in the world just happened. She couldn't just throw out something like getting a job in New Jersey and us looking at new houses and not say something.

"I need your opinion." Her chin rested in her hands and she looked me in the eye.

I stared back. Hard.

"Look at this. You think this should be blue or yellow?"

I came behind her and looked over her shoulder at the screen.

Summer Sale on All Beds
A Honey of a Deal!

"Blue is nice," I said.

"I agree." She clicked on the blue and repositioned a few words before turning to me. I braced for the news. News that we'd have to move to New Jersey and live with Naniji and Nanaji. Instead she said, "When's the last time you cleaned out the microwave?"

Usually the repetition of crochet set a plan into motion in my head. Instead, my thoughts had been stuck in a continuous round like the wristbands I'd been making—the loops forming one big, repeating circle like a spiral. Mom was serious. She'd called her parents. My grandparents whom I'd only seen twice my whole life. Mom never said much about them except that they had high standards and certain expectations—which made Dad clear his throat and find an excuse to leave the room. I only knew they were still alive by the hundred-dollar checks they sent Fran and me on holidays.

Finally, Fran stopped by the store to take me home so Mom and Dad could finish closing up for the day. I threw my bag on the floor the minute I walked inside the house.

"You better pick that up," Fran said.

Whenever Mom wasn't around, Fran just had to pretend she was my mother. I used to think it was a special Fran trait, but I'd seen Brooke treat her younger twin brothers the same way a few times. Older-sister stuff that made me glad I was the younger one. It didn't help that ever since Fran started high school, trying to figure out her moods was like trying to unravel a skein of yarn, in the dark, after a litter of kittens attacked it.

I kicked my bag in the general direction of the hooks I should hang it from. I'd tell Mom it fell.

"Dinner isn't an experiment, is it?" I asked, sitting down at the table in the kitchen.

"It's broccoli pesto with angel hair pasta."

"Can you make me regular spaghetti?"

Fran twisted her light brown hair and flipped it over her shoulder. It fell in an untangled curl like on a shampoo commercial. She complained it was too thin, but I'd do anything for hair that curled and bounced instead of clumped together.

"Maybe your talent for the festival should be being a crybaby," Fran said, grabbing garlic and an armful of other stuff from the fridge.

"For your information, I've always hated angel hair pasta, and why's everyone making such a huge deal over the festival?" The minute the words were out of my mouth, it was like Fran peeling the skin off a clove of garlic—they stunk up the room.

Fran had just pulled a knife from the drawer and turned to look at me. The knife clutched in her right hand made her look dangerous. Not to mention the way the light reflected off her glasses with a glare. Fran had mono the year it was her turn to be in the festival, so she'd never had a chance to be in it. It was probably the only thing in her life she hadn't won.

"There are some things that are bigger than you and what you think is important." Fran turned back to the broccoli. "And maybe the fact that they're giving away two thousand dollars for the talent show should tell you that lots of people are taking this seriously."

"Two thousand dollars? For cheesy dancing and lip-synching?" I got up and grabbed some strawberries from the fridge.

Two thousand dollars was way more than I had saved up from every birthday check from Naniji and it had to be enough to stop Mom from turning her New Jersey idea into an actual plan.

I grabbed Fran's phone and scanned for the message she'd sent Candice earlier with the food pantry schedule.

This is Flor, not Fran.

Meet me tomorrow at the store.

I know what we'll do for our talent.

Chapter Seven

Random Bee Fact #103:
Scouts vote about where to live. If there is talk of moving at least fifteen of the scout bees have to agree. Those who don't agree are head-butted until they do.

After spending the next morning cleaning out the fridge in the break room, Dad had me suit up in the mattress costume. Candice hadn't shown up yet and Fran had her phone at work, so I didn't know when or if she'd come.

"Flor, wave while you're out there," Dad said. "People buy when they feel happy and if we look like a friendly store. Happiness equals . . ."

"Sales?"

"You got it, kiddo!"

Dad's sales mottoes could usually be answered with "Sales" the same way Sunday school questions could be answered with "God."

I'd been outside for all of two minutes when Candice came down the sidewalk. She was far enough away that I could see her clearly through the misplaced eyeholes of the mattress costume. It was when people got too close that I couldn't see who they were.

Even if I hadn't been dressed up like a walking mattress and practically handing Candice a reason for that smirk smeared across her face, I still would have gotten that sweaty stickiness that sent goose bumps up and down my arms. She brought out everything bad in me. I turned into the third-grade version of myself when she was around. The eight-year-old me who'd scrunch up her face and say, "So?" to every mean thing Candice said about me.

"When did your dad start selling maxi pads?" Candice asked.

"Ha, very funny." (My twelve-year-old version of "So?")

"So you have a great idea for our talent?" she asked.

Something about the way she let her voice get all squeaky as she asked me said: *I'm prepared to hear something stupid.*

"Yeah. I have." I swallowed. "You play the piano and

I'll play the recorder." I wasn't going to admit to Candice that I didn't have any other talents.

"A piano-recorder *duet?*"

Candice could take non-mean words and turn them into tiny shards of broken glass that poked you, but didn't hurt until a few seconds later. "Yeah. A duet. Mr. Fitz said my recorder playing was the best in the class."

Candice let out a laugh. "That was in fourth grade."

"Well, I can still play 'Morning' by Edvard Grieg."

"That fact that you even know that song gives me *some* hope," Candice said, blowing hair off her face. "I'll pull out my *beginners* piano books. I'm sure I have a version of 'Morning' in there that will be easy enough for you to play along with me."

Candice stalked off and I sighed at the way she highlighted "some," "beginners," and "easy enough" by stretching the words out like they were bubblegum. My breath was thick and steamy and I couldn't get away from it. A duet with Candice was going to kill me, if the humidity and the stuffiness inside the mattress suit didn't first.

I dug around in my closet until I found the dark blue rectangular case I'd been searching for. My recorder from fourth-grade music class.

Brooke had scoffed at having to learn the recorder. She

called it "the annoying cousin of the flute." *For amateurs,* she'd said. But I'd secretly loved the recorder. I never had patience for the piano or violin—both instruments Fran played well enough to get the distinction awards that lined the bookshelves in the living room.

The recorder was kind of like crochet to me. Easier than other instruments, but once you got the hang of it, it could sound just as good as anything else, the same way more advanced crochet stitches could look just like knit.

I wiped the mouthpiece of the recorder on the bottom of my T-shirt and blew through it. It screeched louder and shriller than I remembered. I flipped through *Recorder Magic: The Classics,* the book that came with the recorder, and brushed up on my finger placement.

Once "Mary Had a Little Lamb" and "Hot Cross Buns" sounded more like how they were supposed to, I flipped to the last song in the book, "Morning" by Edvard Grieg. The advanced songs at the back of the book made me sound like I knew what I was doing.

About the fifteenth time through the song, Dad poked his head into my room.

"What's with the music?" he asked.

"Talent for the festival."

Dad nodded. "I always liked the recorder. It'll definitely be a unique talent."

"There's a two-thousand-dollar prize, you know." I let that hang in the air between us, hoping Dad would say something about the store or Mom's plan or the escalating fight between them. They couldn't think Fran and I had no clue about any of it.

Dad scratched the middle of his chest. The *scritch* of his shirt rubbing against his chest was the only sound in my room.

"Are we moving to New Jersey?" The words came out like I'd snipped each one with a big pair of scissors. Sharp and choppy.

Dad stopped scratching his chest. His whole face, from the skin around his mouth to his eyebrows, it all just kind of slipped farther down his face.

I tried to think of something else to say, like it'd be okay or I didn't mind, but none of that was true.

"So you heard that, huh?" Dad looked at me, his mouth in that weird half smile, half frown that wrinkled his chin. "Listen, Flor. Nothing has been decided yet but . . . I've . . . I've got to go help Fran finish up that dinner. Wash your hands and set the table."

I waited until the carpeted thuds of his footsteps got to the end of the hallway and hit the wood floor in the kitchen, rattling the dishes in the hutch. Our house had that settled, cozy feel. I didn't know what most of the houses in New Jersey were like, but if Naniji's was anything to go by, it would be white carpets and formal dining rooms and no ice cream in front of the television.

Dad said nothing was decided, but the whole idea of moving was like a bad aftertaste that clung to the back of my mind the way roasted red peppers made me burp up the flavor for two days straight.

Chapter Eight

Random Bee Fact #46:
Not all bees and wasps die after stinging you.

The beginning of summer had a slow-motion feel to it. Usually I could enjoy it for the first few weeks before Mom or Dad piled jobs on me and then it'd be the Fourth of July and things fast-forwarded to school starting.

Not this summer.

Candice and I spent another day at Mr. Henry's raking, pulling weeds, and piling wood until the yard finally started to become visible. Then, Candice gave me a practice schedule for our talent. She wanted me to practice at home forty-five minutes every day. Every. Day. I was all for winning this thing, but this seemed excessive.

On top of all the festival stuff, Dad wanted to get his money's worth out of the mattress suit, so I spent any free time suiting up and standing outside the store.

I welcomed the blast of air-conditioning as I walked into the library after spending an hour in the stuffy mattress costume. That thing was like a sauna for ideas—they poured out of me, along with sweat, as I paced up and down the sidewalk. I realized Dad needed some fresh ideas to save his store. After all, he was the one who liked to say, "You can't reinvent what you sell, but you can reinvent the way you sell." He'd been feeding me sales tips since I was two, but it was time to put them into practice.

Staying in Honeydale was going to take more than just winning the title of Queen Bee. I needed to help Dad prove to Mom that he was doing his best at the store. I just hoped Dad would be as excited about my ideas as he'd been about the mattress costume.

I sat at the edge of the computer chair and typed "How to improve your sales" into the search bar, scanning the list of books that matched.

Sales Strategies to Success

10,000 Techniques That Sell, Sell, Sell!

Raising Potential for Rising Sales

Sales Techniques That Work!

The last title sounded the most promising, so I clicked

on it and scribbled down where to find it. I'd never been in the section of the library with all the thick business books. It was quiet and dark, since the shelves were packed without any gaps between the books like in other sections. I had to use two hands to get the book down, but at least it wasn't as big as *10,000 Techniques That Sell, Sell, Sell!* I didn't have time to sift through that many ideas.

I skimmed over the contents page and flipped to chapter four: "What You're Doing Wrong and How to Make it Right."

Even well-established businesses fall into sales slumps. Is your sales slump a blip for the season or has it flatlined? If your sales have been down for months, it's time to take a look at what you're doing wrong and make it right.

You're not offering anything new. The fix: Find new products that go well with your existing products.

Your prices are too low. The fix: Raise prices to meet new demands of the economy.

You're not utilizing social media. The fix: Set up a website and offer online-only deals.

The list went on and on. The chapter ended with:

In order to recharge your sales, you have to make changes. Changes aren't always cheap, but a true salesman knows: You've got to spend money to make money.

When Gramps was still around and no customers came

in for days, I'd ask him how he made any money. He'd say, "A good mattress is an investment. If people bought a mattress every day, I'd be selling a bad product."

Dad's store might not be the kind of place you went into every week like the grocery store, but aside from Mrs. Thorton, no one had come into the store at all for weeks.

You've got to spend money to make money. I'd never heard Dad use that one before. Maybe that's what we needed to do.

I dropped the book on the "Leave books here after browsing" trolley on my way out the door.

When I pushed through the store door Mom waved her arms for me to be quiet and pointed at the phone. I wiggled past her as she "Mm-hmm"ed a few times into the phone.

Dad was in the break room, standing at the outside door that opened into the alley. He quickly stubbed his cigarette against the bricks outside, but he couldn't hide the smoke fast enough. Dad hadn't smoked in years.

I swallowed down my lecture about lung cancer and launched into my idea. "Dad, I think we need to branch out."

"Branch out?" he asked, coughing smoke into his fist, still trying to cover it up.

"Yes, I've been doing some research and I think if we

offer a new product we can attract some new business and get sales up."

Maybe he was just relieved I hadn't said anything about the smoking, but he gestured toward the table and grabbed me a sparkling lemonade from the fridge. "What'd you have in mind?"

Mom hardly ever let me drink the sparkling lemonades, so I quickly took a big sip, enjoying the tingly burn as it made its way down my throat. "Well, it has to be something that would go with mattresses and beds. I was thinking sheets and bedding, or what about dressers and desks?"

Dad nodded and rubbed his chin. "That's a pretty hefty investment if we order entire room sets."

I nodded. "Yes, but sometimes you have to spend money to make money."

Dad laughed, and it was hard to describe just how that felt. Not just making Dad laugh, but making him laugh in a way that meant he was proud of me, not teasing me. "Atta girl, Flor. I told you, you have sales in your blood." He smacked his hands down on the table as he stood up. "Let's see what we can find and get ordering."

"Ordering what?" Mom stood in the doorway, her arms crossed.

"It's about time we expanded the business, Mina." He

reached to put his arm around her, but she slumped out from under him. "Just imagine, our showroom filled with not only beds and mattresses, but desks and dressers, too!"

"Expand the business? Now? Where is this money coming from?"

"Mina," Dad said, "sometimes you've got to spend money to make money." I mouthed the words right along with Dad. He nailed it.

"Spend money, huh?" Mom shook her head. "Or waste money, like buying that ridiculous mattress costume instead of using that same amount of money and time to invest more in advertisements?"

"The mattress *is* an advertisement," Dad argued.

"My parents didn't offer to loan us money so you could buy toys," Mom said.

I slipped out of the break room and clicked around on the computer for wholesale desks, trying to ignore the words Mom and Dad were throwing at each other.

At least no customers meant no one would walk into the middle of their fight.

Chapter Nine

Random Bee Fact #10:
People think that ants are amazing for being able to carry fifty times their weight, but bees can carry 122 times their weight—while flying.

By the time Thursday came, spending time with Candice at Mr. Henry's felt like a day at King's Island compared to being stranded at the store, where Mom and Dad's whispered arguing turned to thick silences, making it stuffier than the inside of the mattress suit. I managed to find a few options for the desks and printed off the manufacturers' websites and e-mails for Dad. He said he'd make some calls and discuss it with Mom once he had all the details ready. I crossed my fingers that Mom would at least listen to him without bringing up Naniji and Nanaji's money.

I didn't want to discuss the desks with Candice in the car, so we drove to Mr. Henry's with Mom's favorite light jazz station playing in the background, making it feel like the longest elevator ride ever instead of a car ride.

Mr. Henry was waiting at the top of his driveway. He didn't even bother with a hello or good morning, just a gruff "I've got an important job for you two."

"That's wonderful," Mom said, smiling and nodding at Candice and me. "I'll be back with lunch."

Why did Mom make so much effort being nice to Mr. Henry, someone we'd only just met, but then to Dad, her own husband, she couldn't even spare a crumb of niceness? Maybe I took Dad's side because Mom treated him the way Fran bossed me.

I watched Mom drive off before turning to Mr. Henry. He was staring at Candice and me. "I need help checking on my hives. Don't want to lose any this year and this leg isn't cooperating."

Even after seeing those burned boxes the other day and smelling the dead bees, it wasn't like there wasn't honey for sale at the grocery store or flowers not blooming. I'd been hearing about bees dying since first grade, but I never knew when things were serious or just hyped up. I mean, I'd learned about global warming my entire life, but we still drove cars filled with gasoline.

"Isn't there medicine for the bees?" I asked.

The plywood ramp wobbled and made a smacking sound against the concrete as Mr. Henry made his way toward us. "No, there isn't medicine. Well, not anything I'd spray on *my* bees. Follow me," he said, not even waiting to see if Candice and I were going to.

"I read up on AFB," Candice said, scrambling to stay alongside Mr. Henry. She turned to me. "That's an abbreviation for American foulbrood—it's the bacteria that killed those bees, leaving that bad smell."

"Duh," I said.

Candice rolled her eyes and turned back to Mr. Henry. "I understand now why you had to burn the hives. AFB can live up to fifty years. I also did some research on mites. They're easier to deal with. If you don't like using chemicals, essential oils like thyme and mint help to get rid of them. I looked up pictures online so I know what to look for to spot signs of mites."

Mr. Henry "hmm"ed, deep and rumbling as he rolled toward the barn. He flipped the latch of the lock up and I shoved myself in front of Candice to help him push open the big door. Inside the barn smelled exactly like the shed behind Gram's house—of dried leaves and gasoline.

Mr. Henry opened and closed some drawers that lined a workbench along one wall.

"Come here and give me a hand," he said.

I rushed to his side before Candice could, wondering what in the world Mr. Henry was looking for. He pulled out a lighter from the drawer and dropped it into his shirt pocket before slamming the drawer shut with his good leg. "Get some of that newspaper." He pointed to a pile under the workbench. Candice quickly reached for it.

Mr. Henry grabbed a can that looked like the oilcan from *The Wizard of Oz* and a flat thing that looked like something you'd use to scrape off paint. He put them in his lap.

"You're going to need those," he said, nodding at two white hats with netting attached around the brim hanging from the wall.

"What for?" I asked.

Candice sighed and grabbed the hats. "To protect our faces." Her voice rose at the end, the way you ask a question—how you say "duh" without actually saying it.

Every time I could feel myself inch ahead of Candice, she'd know something or do something to push herself in front. I'd always thought it had started after third grade, when we'd stopped being friends, but as I snuck looks over at her as Mr. Henry singled out one of the beehives, a big white box at the end of the last row, and I listened to Candice spout facts about mites and bee viruses and their possible solutions, I could remember always feeling a step or two behind her in kindergarten and first grade, too. It wasn't just that I felt like I was trailing behind, it was almost like Candice only liked me when I was.

After I won a coloring contest for our school-wide antibullying campaign in first grade, she didn't even congratulate me when the principal announced the winners like the rest of the class. She just leaned over and said the competition was babyish. And in second grade I made it to the final three in the PE jump-rope contest and afterward she stopped playing jump-rope games, declaring sitting on top of the monkey bars watching the boys play kickball at recess was more fun.

Maybe because she wasn't Fran and I didn't live with her I could put up with the way she ignored and made fun of things for as long as I did, but something about the way she kept pushing herself to the front with Mr. Henry left me feeling like one of those bee mites. Something she wanted to better.

Mr. Henry clicked the lighter a few times before lighting a handful of newspaper and stuffing it into the oilcan-looking thing. Almost immediately smoke poured out. He closed the lid and held the can near the white box, squeezing an accordion type of handle at the side, spreading smoke out over the hive. "This'll calm them. You'll have no trouble pulling out a few frames. They'll burrow down and focus on eating honey, won't even give you much notice." He pointed at the white hive boxes, but I still had no idea what a frame was.

I took a few steps closer to the boxes, hoping whatever a frame was would suddenly make sense. I wanted to do something before Candice proved just how much more she knew than me.

Candice stepped forward, the netted hat covering her face, but her arms and hands stayed bare. She placed her bare hand on top of the hive. "It's okay. I know what to look for. I read up on this after our first visit and found some videos online."

"Oh, I'm not nervous," I said, plopping the other bee hat on top of my head, quickly tucking the netting into the neck of my T-shirt like Candice had. "I just didn't think we'd pull the frames out yet. I mean . . ." I tried to think of something intelligent to say, but I didn't know the first thing about bees other than that they made honey. The fact Candice was maybe even good at this bee thing made my skin get that too-tight-and-itchy feel. "Shouldn't we check around the hive first?"

"For what?" Candice rolled her eyes. "Actually, why don't you start, Flor? You seem to know how it's done."

That little hint of guilt for hating Candice just for

knowing more than me was washed away by the tidal wave of annoyance at the way she wasn't just a know-it-all, but she was a know-it-all for the sake of making me feel like chewed gum squished under a chair.

I swallowed hard and stood across from her, the white box between us buzzing with an energy that made me feel like I needed to catch my breath, but in an excited, less nervous way. I put my hand on the hive, surprised at the warmth and the slight hum of movement that spread through my hand and up to my elbow. Candice knew a lot about bees, but that didn't mean I couldn't learn.

Not sure how to open the stainless-steel lid, I looked for any kind of handle. At least a dozen bees hovered in and out of a hole at the side of the hive, but there weren't any other places big enough to put your hand to open the box. It could be as easy as lifting off the steel lid by grabbing it at the sides, but what if the bees escaped in an angry cloud of buzzing stingers?

"I thought so," Candice said, shouldering her way in front of me. She lifted off the silver cover and leaned it against the hive before putting her hand right through a rectangular cutout in the middle of a second lid made of wood.

I leaned over her shoulder to see what was inside. Ten wooden slats were lined up like slices of bread.

Sunlight poured into the hive. I watched as the bees wiggled through the gaps that ran between the pieces of wood.

"Move," Candice growled, pushing me with her hip as she set the wooden lid next to the steel one against the hive.

Mr. Henry used the flat paint scraper to pry up one of the pieces of wood. "This here is a frame."

He held up a large rectangle filled with honeycomb, bees, and glistening honey for a few seconds before gently dropping the frame back into place.

"To pull out a frame, you take this hive tool and work it like so." He stuck the flat part under the wood of the frame and levered it so the frame lifted slightly before letting it drop back into the box, scattering the bees that'd been hovering.

I held my hand out for the hive tool, determined to do this before Candice could. I watched the rows of frames for several seconds, trying to find one that had no bees near it. The bees didn't seem to follow any sort of pattern. I couldn't predict which frames the bees would climb out of next.

After counting to ten, I reached slowly for a frame at the end. I figured if I only disturbed a frame on the end, it'd cause less of a chain reaction than if I reached in and pulled out the middle frame.

I dug the hive tool under the wooden rim at the middle of the frame and twisted my wrist like opening a can of soda. Two bees wiggled out of the frame and bumped against my hand. I froze, afraid they'd sting, but they flew away. It was like they were sniffing me the way dogs do. Maybe they didn't smell a threat on me and had decided to move on.

Mr. Henry brought the smoking can closer to the hive and let the smoke spread out over the frames. I inhaled, careful to let my breath seep slowly out of my mouth. It was partly because of the smoke, but partly because it took a lot of effort to keep my hands from shaking. My fingers squeezed around the handle of the hive tool and pulled on it gently till I could gauge how much strength I needed to pull it out. The frame was heavy. Only when I had the frame almost completely out did I realize why. The thing was packed full of bees. Who knew something so small could add up to weigh so much when they were all clumped together?

The hexagon pattern of the hive and the constant movement of the bees reminded me of the Where's Waldo? books I'd pore over when I was little. There was so much to see you couldn't take it all in at once.

I held the frame half in, half out and watched as the sunlight hit the orangey liquid and made the white box behind us glow yellow. The hive was a crisscross of cardboard-looking walls of honeycomb. Some of the tiny hexagons were darker than others and some bulged and looked like they'd been filled with yellow shaving cream.

"Hold it straight up and look here." Mr. Henry locked the wheels of his wheelchair and pushed himself up, leaning on his good leg. With his bare finger, he touched the hexagons that were filled with the golden shaving cream. The bees crawled around his finger like it was just another piece of their home. "These cells are full of bees about to hatch. The eggs are these." He moved his finger over to brown hexagons with what looked like tiny pieces of rice inside. "Those eggs will turn into white worms and then to the yellow crusty cells before they emerge as bees. These"—he held his hand out for the hive tool and scraped at a big lump of honeycomb that rose from the rest like a hill—"are like bridges the bees make so they can go across the frames instead of up and over. I don't always scrape them off, but if I leave it too long, it'll be difficult to harvest the honey in the fall when all the frames are stuck together. Now go ahead and put her back in gently."

I held the frame over the empty slot. The bees continued to clamber all over each other, only a few finding my hands interesting. The frame slid in easily. Letting go of the frame left a sudden stillness all over my skin, making my arm hair stand up straight.

"We'll check each of the frames in these boxes carefully," Mr. Henry said.

"But what are we looking for? What tells us the hive is sick?" I asked.

Candice sighed. She'd been sighing so much she was going to run out of oxygen. "The bees should be moving around. Some cells should be darker, almost brown; that means there's honey. Anything dried out or smelly is bad."

Mr. Henry nodded along. "You've done your research."

Candice could keep pretending to be some kind of bee whisperer to Mr. Henry all she wanted, but I was the one who lifted the frame. I stuck the hive tool under the next frame and lifted. The heaviness of the moving bees swarming on the frame strained my arm in that way running burns your lungs, but in that good-pain way you feel you're getting stronger.

Chapter Ten

Random Bee Fact #27:
Large companies should study bees to learn effective
management and organizational styles.

The next morning Fran pushed a plate of chia-and-
oatmeal pancakes topped with fruit toward me.

No syrup.

Two blueberries dotted the middle like eyes, strawberries arched out like hair, and thin slices of banana fanned
out in a too-happy smile.

Fran leaned across the table and added a dollop of
whipped cream on each side like foamy ears and tried to
smile. Her smile looked too similar to the bananas—like
someone had pulled her lips up like that, putting them in
that position without her permission.

"Whipped coconut cream," she said.

Even the whipped cream was fake. Well, Fran would argue it was more real than the stuff from a can I preferred, but the only time I liked the taste of coconut was when Brooke's mom made us kid piña coladas at slumber parties. We didn't say anything, but we both heard it.

I knew Fran was trying to make me feel better about overhearing Mom and Dad last night. Mom had bought a plane ticket to check out houses in New Jersey around Naniji and Nanaji in two weeks. She said she'd put a lot of thought into all of it. And she had an interview date set at the private school she'd attended growing up. If she got the job as an art teacher, Fran and I'd have our tuition covered. She flung all the plans and details at Dad, how we'd live with Naniji until Dad could settle things with the store and join us. Nanaji owned a big company and Mom said they'd be able to find a position for Dad. Dad hadn't said much until then, but once Mom mentioned the job with Nanaji, Dad's voice got loud and edged with a roughness that felt like he was trying not to yell.

That's when Fran had come in and pulled me back to her room. A tinge of softness that Fran actually remembered how thin the walls were between Mom and Dad's room and mine chipped through the frustration that'd been building up like a brick wall, piece by piece, inside of me. Instead of letting the softness expand and start to crumble away at my frustration, I tried to hold on to it and let it harden because I wanted to be angry.

Before Dad decided to help Gramps with the mattress store, he worked as a lawyer. I was pretty small, but I remember him wearing a tie, and sometimes we didn't see him until early morning because he stayed so late at work. Then Dad quit to help Gramps at the store. Dad didn't have such long hours and Mom was happy. *Was.*

Overnight, moving had become more than just an idea Mom talked about. It had turned into a plan.

I swallowed down as much of my smiling pancake as I could, wishing it would fill me with happiness instead of the weird lump that'd formed in my chest.

"We'll leave at eleven to go to the food pantry," Fran said, taking my plate.

I hid in my closet and practiced the recorder until the squishy parts at the tops of my fingers had permanent circles indented into them. My elbows banged into the walls on either side of me, but it was the best way to avoid having to see Mom. Plus, Candice and I were going to practice our duet after we helped Fran with the food pantry. I might have overexaggerated my abilities to play, but I was more determined than ever to sound good so Candice would know I was serious about the festival and deserved to be here as much as her. Plus, if I could actually play, we'd have a chance at winning.

After I saw Mom's car leave for morning art classes, I went out to the kitchen to wait for Fran. Mom had left the festival schedule on the counter, another one of her not-so-subtle reminders that I needed to fill in the family calendar. I grabbed a stack of Post-its and stuck the upcoming events on the calendar. The talent showcase was coming up, and then we had the nursing home luncheon. There were other smaller events at the library, Candice's orchard, and the camp. I stuck on Post-its for Mr. Henry's and the food pantry and then stuck on even more for dressing up as a mattress and cleaning the store. I made sure each day had at least three Post-its even if some of them just said "shower."

Fran walked in, immediately looking over my shoulder. "What are you wearing for the talent showcase?"

"Regular clothes," I said, shrugging.

"Flor, you can't go in looking like you pulled your outfit out of the Lost and Found."

I looked down at my T-shirt I'd cut with the collar slightly wider and my longer denim shorts I'd stitched on a few crocheted circles I'd made with yarn scraps. "It's called being yourself, Fran. You should try it sometime, instead of always trying to be my mom."

"I'm trying to help you, not boss you around." Fran

flipped open her water bottle and leaned against the counter, then paused. "Do you think she'll get the job?"

I shrugged. No matter what, I couldn't picture Mom teaching at some fancy school, Fran and me wearing plaid uniforms and living with Naniji and Nanaji. Mom had worked at the gallery, giving art classes to old ladies and little kids since I could remember. And Honeydale public schools were all I knew.

If Mom did get the job, private school uniforms would be the least of my worries.

I stood outside the church waiting for Candice while Fran went inside to get the ovens turned on. It was only a few minutes later when I saw her coming down the sidewalk. The dimple on her left cheek reminded me of the time we'd watched *Anne of Green Gables* in first grade. When Anne told Diana that she would do anything to have her dimples, I looked over at Candice and envied that dimple for the very first time in my life. I never even knew I should want a dimple before that.

When I told Candice about it she'd laughed and said I was super skinny like Anne, but at least I had Diana's long ebony hair. I didn't know yet that "ebony" was just another word for black. I loved the idea that my hair could be described with a word that sounded special.

"Have you been waiting forever?" Candice asked.

"No, we just got here a few minutes ago."

"My mom had me empty out the dishwasher at the café," Candice said, shaking her head. "You get it."

I nodded because I did. Dad's motto was something along the lines of: *Why pay someone to do something you can get your child to do for free!* Notice the exclamation point is *not* a question mark. Then he'd go on to say something like: *When I was your age and my dad started this place_____.* Fill in the blank with whatever I was complaining about: taking out the trash, cleaning the endless windows and mirrors, whatever, then, multiply by ten. My dad liked me to think his life was much more difficult than mine.

A déjà vu kind of feeling tugged at me, reminding me that Candice and I had more in common than I wanted to admit.

I rushed Candice inside the church, not sure how I felt about this reminder of a connection with her. In a way it was nice because Brooke was away and most of my other friends from coding club were school friends that I didn't really hang out with outside of school. Candice hopped down the steps next to me as we made our way into the basement. When she was like this—chatty and practically skipping—I could imagine being friends.

Fran had already emptied one shelf and was dusting

when we walked in. "Rags are over there. Be sure you only empty one shelf at a time and line the cans up so the closest to reaching the expiration date are at the front and newer cans at the back. I don't want anything to go to waste."

We dusted and organized as Fran set out the newly donated cans from a large container. "I'm going to get started on the casseroles."

I picked up the next stack of cans. "Does anyone eat water chestnuts?"

"Oh, that just gave me an idea for a stir-fry," Fran said from the kitchen.

I wiped off the lids before sliding them back in place on the shelves, reminding myself not to mention any of the other strange foods I saw that'd been somehow preserved into a can.

Soon the entire church basement was filled with the smells of Fran's tuna-and-yam cream-of-mushroom casserole. As Fran wiped up the counters, she explained that the food pantry was one of the only places in town that families in need could stock up on basics. I felt bad for turning my nose up at the powdered milk when I'd stocked the shelf.

After topping the casserole with crushed-up cornflakes and dried herbs, Fran made us each taste a bite so we knew what we were offering to the people who came. It actually tasted okay.

Most of the people who came in were older, but a few moms with little kids came in. The kids gobbled down the bowls of food we offered them and the moms shyly took the recipes.

Fran shooed us upstairs to practice for the showcase when it was time to lock up. I grabbed my recorder and followed Candice to the sanctuary. Her mom was in the church choir and got permission for us to practice with the church piano.

This was the first time we'd be practicing together.

"Okay, Flor. I'll lead with an intro and I want you to come in at about count four. Make sense?"

"Yep." I pulled my recorder out of its case and held it up in front of me. I could read notes, but counts? I didn't know what Candice was talking about. I let her start playing and when I thought it sounded like I should start playing, I did.

"Uh, I said on four." Candice shook her head and played the beginning again, plunking it out loud and clear with one hand and tapping her leg with the other. "One and two and three and four." She nodded at me and I started playing.

I was screechy. Candice was plunky, which she blamed on my bad timing.

After thirty minutes of practicing, any tiny sense I'd

felt that the wedge between us was shrinking evaporated.

This was hopeless. The whole thing reminded me of a really cool advanced crochet project, where I focused on how it would look at the end, not even thinking about all the difficult stitches needed to get there.

Each moment with Candice was like a difficult stitch I had to work and unravel, making it difficult to remember what I was even trying to make.

Chapter Eleven

Random Bee Fact #32:
Bees are less likely to sting if they've just eaten.

Fran and I walked through the back door at home and were hit with the smell of onions so strong my eyes watered. It took a minute for the comforting smell of potato, bread, and burned butter to mix in with the overpowering smell of onions.

Aloo parathas!

I kicked off my shoes and ran into the kitchen. Fran hadn't used butter in any of our meals for months and I had to fight the urge to run over to Mom and lick the parathas she'd piled on a plate next to a pot of simmering chicken curry.

The last time Mom put this much effort into cooking

was when she wanted Dad to build a shed to store his overflowing golf club collection. The time before that was when she had to convince all of us to be her subjects for a project she did for her psychology class back when she wanted to be a life coach.

It might have smelled like chicken curry and aloo parathas, but what it really smelled like was a mom bribe.

"Hey, girls," Mom called, flipping a steaming paratha onto a plate. "You're home early. I've got dinner covered and the table set. Help yourselves to some mango lassi while I add a few last-minute touches."

Fran sat across from me. Neither of us touched anything. The mango lassi was in an etched glass pitcher Mom kept in the hutch. I didn't even know you could really use it. I thought it was just for looks since she'd never gotten it out before. Not even the year Nanaji and Naniji came and made a big deal out of celebrating Diwali.

"Mmm, mmm, mmm," Dad said, walking through the back door. "Dinner's smelling good, ladies."

"Dad. That's so chauvinistic." Fran's water glass clunked onto the table, making the silverware rattle together.

"Just in time, dear. Everything's on the table." Mom flitted and chirped like one of those annoying birds outside your bedroom window on a Saturday morning.

Dad dug into a huge scoop of pilau rice and a paratha as Mom set the rest of the food on the table. She didn't even stop him like she normally would, reminding him that his metabolism wasn't like it used to be. Fran poked at her rice and I ripped my paratha into tiny pieces, my fingers bright pink from the still-hot potato filling and shiny from the butter.

Since Mom wasn't nagging any of us, I added an extra slice of butter to my plate and dipped my shredded paratha into it.

"It's nice all of us being here, having a family dinner," Mom said, flattening her cloth napkin across her lap.

"Sure is." Dad stuffed another bite into his mouth.

Was he really so oblivious that Mom was buttering us up more than I'd buttered up my paratha?

"Girls, you've barely touched your food," Mom said. Her eyebrows dipped into a suspicious V. "Fran, I made the mutter tofu especially for you."

Dad looked up and noticed the barely touched food on our plates. "Girls, your mom put a lot of effort into this meal—you should eat."

"Really, Dad?" Fran asked. "When's the last time Mom made dinner?"

"Fran," Mom said, her napkin now scrunched in her fist on the table. "I've gladly given up some of my kitchen duty this summer so you could work on your recipes for the food pantry. Why can't I just make something special when I feel like it?"

"So, you're *just* making a special dinner? No special announcement to go with it?" Fran did that weird thing with her jaw that she usually reserved for making a tell-the-truth face at me.

"Yeah. I thought you had to put family meetings on the calendar," I said, and shoved pratha into my mouth.

"This isn't a family meeting, it's dinner. Why are you two making this difficult?"

I chewed slowly and stared down at my plate.

Mom pushed her plate back. "Fine. I've purchased a plane ticket to New Jersey and I leave in two weeks. I've already been short-listed after the phone interview with St. Hilda's Academy. It's a great school and you girls' tuition will be covered. . . ."

Fran gripped her mango lassi so tight the liquid wobbled inside the glass. "Maybe if you and Dad fought quieter this would all come as a shock."

Mom's mouth opened and closed, but no words escaped.

"The only thing you haven't bothered to explain is *why*. Why now? It's my senior year. I have a life!" Fran crumpled into her chair.

My anger at Mom squished into sadness and sat heavy between my throat and chest. Fran's emotions tended to be more along the annoyance and frustration side of the spectrum. I rarely saw her get *upset*-upset like she'd cry.

Mom cleared her throat and glanced over at Dad's plate, not actually looking at him. "Okay. Well, now, because things haven't been going well at the store for the past year despite my"—she cleared her throat and flung her hand in Dad's direction—"*our* best efforts, things aren't getting better fast enough. Art teaching jobs don't come up often and I'd love it if you girls got to go to St. Hilda's like I did."

Fran started to interrupt Mom, but Mom put her hand up. "I know it's your senior year. I know it'll be difficult, but I'd never do this if I didn't think it'd be for the best. New Jersey isn't that different. . . ." Mom's voice trailed off as she watched Fran stalk past her.

Mom sighed, her eyes on me.

"I'm not hungry," I said, pushing away from the table.

I thought she might call me back, but all I heard her say was, "That's enough rice, Kingsley. Your metabolism isn't what it used to be."

Chapter Twelve

Random Bee Fact #31:
A bee all alone has many predators. Bees all together
surround attacking insects and cook them to death with
the heat they create wiggling and fluttering their wings.

The night before the talent showcase my fingers were tired and sore. I wove the loose tail of black yarn in and out of the stitches along the wrist of the fingerless gloves I'd just made and tucked in the last little bit so you couldn't even tell it was there. I didn't always take such care to finish my projects, but after practicing with Candice and Mom announcing she was going to New Jersey no matter what, I reconsidered Fran's suggestion that I should take the whole outfit thing seriously.

I pulled out a black skirt I'd worn a few times that used

to be Fran's and a simple gray T-shirt. My black fingerless gloves would set off the whole recorder-playing thing. I fell asleep actually looking forward to the talent showcase.

The next morning Mom knocked on my door, opening it at the same time.

"Be ready at nine sharp," she said. Her eyes traveled around my room. Something about watching her look around my room highlighted every messy thing about it.

I'd pretty much ignored the piles of laundry and yarn and books since summer started. During the school year Mom checked if my bed was made, but she'd been busier lately and I'd left my door closed most of the time.

I'd never been a neat freak like Fran, but the piles of toppled laundry were scattered in so many places I couldn't remember which ones were clean and which ones weren't.

Mom's mouth opened and closed, but she didn't say anything. Maybe she was all yelled out.

"You need to eat something." Her words squeezed out like others were fighting to come out faster and louder. The real things she wanted to say to me. She closed her eyes and exhaled before turning and walking away.

Inside the car, I rolled down my window, hoping that when I did, the weirdness between Mom and Dad would have somewhere to escape instead of squishing all of us against the dark blue seats and farther away from one another.

"Flor, the air-conditioning is on. Close your window," Mom snapped.

"She just wants some fresh air, Mina," Dad said. He reached toward her hand on the steering wheel.

Mom jerked her hand away from him and the car swerved along with it. "Kingsley, I could crash the car. Why'd you do that?"

"To be nice to you? I don't know." Dad slammed back in his seat, making it strain against the locked position it was in, like if he pushed any harder it'd fling back into my lap.

Mom hadn't even come to a complete stop in front of the high school when I jumped out, ignoring her call to be careful, probably followed by a reminder of what time Dad would be picking me up. I wasn't a baby. I'd heard her this morning.

A few teachers lingered in the halls wearing shorts and flip-flops. It was even weirder seeing teachers dressed like that in school than it was seeing them with their kids at the grocery store.

Thankfully, I knew where the auditorium was because it's where they held sixth-grade graduation. The bottom of my shoe caught on the red carpeting as I walked down the slope between rows of theater seating toward the stage. I clutched my recorder tighter as I got closer to the group clustered at the front. Something about the way they moved, hovering near the long table at the front row but scattering in clumps here and there, reminded me of the bees at Mr. Henry's. The memory of the vibration of the bees when I'd lifted the frames pulsed through my arms. But I could only feel it when I was really still.

As I stood there, waiting to take that step from being far enough back that no one had noticed me yet, to being close enough to the front where the registration table was, I could feel the hum of wings beat like tiny hearts along my arms, giving me goose bumps. I scanned the group at the front for Candice. We were kind of like Fran's soy milk in Dad's hot coffee—smooth as long as you stirred it around, but the minute you turned your back it became sour curdles. Candice had been okay as long as we were busy, but when there was nothing else to distract us from each other, things got bad.

My gloves helped me grip the blue plastic cover of the recorder as I took a deep breath and walked toward the registration table.

"Morning, Florence. Come and get registered." Mrs. Thorton handed me a paper with the number twenty-three printed in thick black smelly marker and a safety pin poked through the top. "Fasten this to the front of your shirt. Everyone will be called in order. Good luck."

She repeated the instructions to someone behind me. I looked around, not sure where to stand or if I should just sit down.

The conversations around me could only be described using a word I learned from Brooke: "crescendo." As more people piled into the auditorium, it started to fill every quiet space. I sat on my hands until they were suctioned and the itchy carpet feel of the seats felt like spikes digging into my palms. I wished I had my own phone so I could message Brooke right then. I'd sent her the wristbands at camp, but hadn't heard from her yet.

Sitting around watching and waiting as the seats around me filled up with girls was a flashback right back to third grade. Nearly two hundred of us had stood still in four straight lines as we waited to hear who won. Candice had been standing next to me in her light pink dress with a ruffled skirt that was so fluffy it pushed against my leg even though I was an arm's length away from her.

I'd stood there, picking at my white gloves, dying to scratch my hair, but there was so much hairspray on it that when I scratched, my entire hair moved, making me itch more. Mom had forced me to wear white tights, too. They were sagging at the crotch and I wanted so badly to give them a good yank that I didn't even hear them call my name. It was only when Candice grabbed my arm and pushed me toward the front—actually, not even then—that I realized they were calling me. Candice jumped up and down and walked me to the front. They put sashes on both of us, mine saying *Little Miss Honeybee* with blue sequins and Candice's saying *Honeybee Court* in the same sequins, and I finally realized that I'd won. It wasn't even something I'd considered when I entered. I thought I'd just get to wear a dress and ride on Gramps's car.

Candice got a simple crown that was lost in her overly poofed and sprayed hair. My crown was taller and had more fake diamonds. When Mrs. Thorton pushed it on my head, the plastic combs at the sides dug into my scalp.

It was fine at first. Candice and I dressed up and went to other festivals. We rode together on the front of every one of Gramps's restored cars. But, halfway through the school year, Candice started to act different. And we'd stopped being friends.

Digging up those memories surprised me in a not-good-surprise kind of way. Like how I'd found Mom's month-old salad behind the flat bottle of Sprite yesterday at the store when she told me to clean the break room fridge. I hadn't been looking for it, I just happened to uncover it. I could just leave it there, pretend I hadn't found it, but it'd only get slimier. I could also just throw it away, but every time Mom brought salad to work, I'd think of that slimy goo I'd found. Candice could be nice to me now, but in that dark corner of my mind, right behind the flat Sprite, there'd always be the reminder of what she'd done and could do again.

Candice arrived and I waved her over. She sat next to me, her sheet music in a folder, but didn't say a word to me.

Mrs. Thorton walked onstage and held the microphone until the auditorium was quiet. "Remember, ladies, this is just a screening. We're checking that you've all chosen acceptable talents. The volunteers joining me up here will be at the festival and helping set up for the performances. The actual judges won't see your talents until that night. So, without wasting any more time, let's get started."

When Mrs. Thorton and the other volunteers were settled at the table in front of the stage, nervousness pushed down on me, making me feel Velcroed to the seat.

The first few talents were dance routines by some younger girls. Then, Carissa Williams walked onstage, swishing her long brown hair over her shoulder. She took a seat at the center of the stage. Carissa was Fran's age. She'd been queen that year and was Fran's rival at school. They alternated as top of class since eighth grade.

Her outfit was terrible—all black and yellow with a headband of bobbling antennae. "Hi, I'm Carissa. I'll be playing the guitar and singing."

I wanted to roll my eyes, but then she started playing. It was folksy and sounded like some band Dad was a fan of. Behind her the words of the song popped up on a projection screen in a way that looked like she'd plucked them out of the guitar itself. I should have thought of that for our talent. It was a simple coding program we'd used in club.

Carissa's voice was the deep and clear kind where you could understand each word in a way it felt like you were the only one in the room. Mrs. Thorton and her volunteers were on their feet singing along and applauding at the end.

"Number twenty-three!" rang through the speakers as the applause for Carissa died down. Candice and I stood up. She barely glanced at me as she started down the aisle. I squeezed my stomach in tighter and tighter with each step up to the stage. I took the recorder out of its pouch and leaned toward the microphone.

"Hi. I'm Florence." The microphone screeched and I flinched at my voice bouncing back at me. "This is Candice." I held my arm out toward the piano. I couldn't remember what else I was supposed to say, so I hitched the recorder up in front of me, happy the fingerless gloves absorbed most of the sweat from my palms, and placed my fingers over the holes. I closed my eyes and waited for Candice to start playing. The first few notes came out screechy before I got into the rhythm.

The slow and fast of the notes reminded me again of a double crochet stitch. It's slow to find the next loop to insert your hook into, then a quick double wrap around the hook and a slowdown to twist and pull the hook through. Over and over.

I hit every note, but it was as shrill and screechy as it had sounded in church. The smattering of clapping after our last notes only proved that I wasn't imagining just how terrible the performance was.

"That was lovely. Next. Twenty-four," Mrs. Thorton called.

Several more people went up, performing everything from gymnastics to Hula-Hoop. But, after hearing Carissa's singing, I wasn't sure we stood a chance.

Things stayed pretty crappy the rest of the day. Dad had me suit up in the mattress when we got to the store, even though the tourist traffic was mostly moms and kids there to visit the train decorated to look like Thomas for the week, not to buy beds or mattresses. A few moms had me pose with their kids. I lost count of how many of them poked and punched the costume.

When I came inside for lunch, Mom held out her phone toward me. "Brooke messaged you about those wristbands you sent her."

I grabbed the phone from her, turning my back to read the text Mom had obviously already read. Under a grainy photo of the orange wristbands and her leather bracelets decorating her arms was a message:

Yay!! Love these. You should send more.

Everyone wants to know where I got them!

I could help you sell them.

Miss you.

It should have felt good to know that complete strangers liked what'd I'd made, but knowing I needed a better talent shadowed even good news with gray. I settled on a kissy face as a response. It was easier to let an emoji talk when I couldn't come up with the words to say.

Chapter Thirteen

Random Bee Fact #72:
Worker bees only live six to eight weeks in the summer.
Most common cause of death: wearing out their wings.

Another week passed, filled with trips to Mr. Henry's to paint his fence and to the food pantry to help Fran, followed by more practicing with Candice. When I brought up the projection idea to her, she'd shrugged and told me to give it a try as long as it didn't interfere with my practice time.

It was starting to feel like I had two nagging older sisters. At least when Fran was being nice, she was really, really nice. It was the same when she was mean. There was never any in-between. But you knew what to expect with her. Candice, on the other hand, was more like a pinwheel, constantly spinning from mean to nice to know-it-all in a single interaction.

Thankfully Fran was in a nice mood and helped me get ready for the first public festival event, a luncheon for the nursing home residents.

We settled on one of her sleeveless button-downs with a skirt that she insisted was the exact mix of casual and classy for a lunch event. She even let me borrow her arrow-shaped earrings.

Dad was quiet as he drove me to Otterbein, the same nursing home Great-Gram had lived at and that Gramps refused to ever be sent to.

Inside held the same smell it had when I used to visit Great-Gram in kindergarten. I used to hold my breath until I got to her room, where it smelled like her perfume and lipstick.

I wanted to turn around and get back in the car, but Dad pulled away without looking back at me. I walked through the big foyer doors. The whole place felt smaller, the ceilings lower. Only the smell was the same.

I made my way down the hall to a long table that had been decorated with a yellow cloth and huge vase of sunflowers that were littered with at least a dozen fake wire bees.

"Hello, Florence," Mrs. Thorton said, waving me over.

"Go on inside the activity room and help get the rest of the tables covered in tablecloths and set up the napkins and plates. The residents will be ready for lunch soon."

She turned back to a small group of ladies, some of whom were the volunteers at the talent showcase, and I slipped into the activity room. It wasn't dotted with the usual small tables set up with games and puzzles, but lined with five long rows of tables with at least ten chairs to a table.

"You with the festival?" a lady with a hairnet and pale green jacket asked.

I nodded and she piled a stack of napkins into my arms.

"Fold those in half and place one to the right of each plate."

For the next half hour, I had a roomful of people telling me what to do and where to put things, and it was almost a relief when Candice arrived. We didn't pay much attention to each other, but continued to work the same way we had for the past week: next to each other without talking.

"Morning, girls." Carissa plopped a fancy centerpiece onto the table that looked like a miniature version of the fake-fuzzy-wire-bees-and-sunflower arrangement at the front, but with a beeswax candle in the middle. "Your guys' duet was super cute," she said.

I squinted at her, trying to figure out if she was making fun of us.

"It was so ironic the way you played up the third grade-ness with the recorder and did that whole then-and-now thing. Really smart."

"Thanks?" I said.

Carissa laughed and hurried off to drop another centerpiece at the next table.

"She was kidding," Candice said. "I knew the duet was a stupid idea."

Before I could remind her that she hadn't come up with any other ideas, Mrs. Thorton clapped her hands from the front of the room. "Ladies, ladies, attention, please." She paused as we quieted down.

"I need at least two of you at a table. You'll plate the food for the residents and refill their drinks. We'll be serving three courses and coffee and tea at the end with a slice of cake. This luncheon is a chance for you queen bees to exercise your worker-bee wings. Let's be abuzz with cheerfulness as we serve." Mrs. Thorton even put her fingers at the sides of her mouth like she was pulling it into a smile.

We placed the last few napkins on the table as the room started to fill up with residents and nurses and wheelchairs and walkers.

I pulled out chairs for the residents at our table and

Candice helped them unfold their napkins and asked them what they wanted to drink. As the food began to come out of the kitchen on trolleys, I went to start putting the soup on the table, only to have Candice move in my way.

For the entire first course we each tried to be the first to do whatever needed done. I'd pick up a fallen napkin, but she'd show up with a fresh one just as I was about to give the one I'd picked up to the resident. I'd ask one their name only to have Candice already call the others by theirs. It's not like our serving skills were being judged. Candice couldn't do anything without doing it better than everyone else. Although, if I was being honest, she *was* good at serving. All that practice helping her mom at the café paid off. She could juggle three plates on one arm and still remember names. All I could do after hanging around Dad's store was clean refrigerators and wear a costume without suffocating.

I stacked the empty soup bowls as the first of the trolleys for the second course came out of the kitchen. Candice grabbed a trolley and plated up the second course before I could put the bowls down and return the dirty dishes to the trolley for the kitchen staff to take away.

That was it. There were moments over the past few weeks where I'd let myself think we could maybe even get along, but she just had to make everything about her and how much better, faster, and smarter she was than me.

I grabbed a bowl of mashed potatoes. "Here, Ms. Lambert," I said, reaching over Candice and her plate of sliced ham. "Have some yummy potatoes." I scooped a spoonful on to her plate and moved on to Mrs. Nelson.

"How about some more lemonade?" Candice asked, squeezing me out of the way.

After adding a scoop of potatoes to Mr. Zander's plate, I purposely turned on my heels and Candice nearly toppled over me. The lemonade in her jug sloshed up the side, but didn't spill over.

"Watch it," she said.

"No. *You* watch it," I said through clenched teeth. "I'm doing what I'm supposed to. Why don't you stop hanging right behind me?"

"It's not third grade anymore, Florence. Stop acting like a baby."

Candice rolled her eyes and tried to step around me. I stepped in front of her. "You're right. It's not third grade anymore, and I'm not too afraid to tell you how I really feel."

"Oh my gosh, you make such a big deal about everything," Candice huffed, and shook her head.

I'd spent third and fourth grade questioning that very thing—if I was or wasn't making a big deal out of what she said about me. Things like "You only won because you're mixed" or "They had to choose you because they are forced to choose someone of color nowadays." A burn behind my heart spread down my arms and up my face before settling directly behind my eyes, making me wonder if I was making it into something bigger. Like it was just a small piece of gum that I was blowing up into a huge bubble filled with air—an unseen kind of thing that doesn't look like it's hurting anyone. So I kind of let all those comments hang over me, invisible and silent, but heavy.

"You don't get it, Candice." The words sprayed out of my mouth, spreading wide and far, silencing the room. Only the old lady playing the piano seemed not to notice.

"I've pretended everything you said didn't really matter, but it does. I'm not making a big deal; you're being *mean*." I scooped up a huge spoonful of potatoes and piled them on Mr. Zander's plate without even asking him if he wanted more.

Candice's mouth was set into a straight line, not smiling and not frowning. She poured more lemonade for Mr. Zander. I pulled my elbow back, my arms full of the bowl of potatoes, at the same time Candice lifted the jug away from Mr. Zander's cup, hitting my arm. The room had finally started to fill with the sprinkle of conversation just as the bowl of mashed potatoes toppled from my arms and hit the beeswax candle in the middle of the table.

In less than a second the fuzzy bees and fake flowers went from bright yellow to a full-out orange flame.

Candice jumped back, hugging the jug of lemonade to her chest. Mr. Zander sipped his lemonade, watching the flame as it spread across the centerpiece the way people watch golf—quiet and slow, moving his head to follow it.

I did the first thing that came to mind and blew on the flame like it was a giant birthday candle. The flame spread to the tablecloth.

"That was stupid. It made it worse," Candice said, her voice both a whisper and a screech.

Mr. Zander dabbed his mouth with a napkin and held out his cup to me. "Maybe you could dump this on it."

I snatched the cup from him and dumped it on the fire, but it only sizzled out a small part on the tablecloth; the centerpiece glowed blue as the flames turned the fuzzy bees into charred wisps of smoke.

I grabbed for the jug in Candice's arms. Her eyes were so wide, I could see the orange glow of the fire in them. She pulled the jug toward herself.

"Give it," I said, yanking on the handle

She relaxed her grip and I flung the entire jug onto the centerpiece, splashing lemonade everywhere.

The lemonade hissed as it hit the fire and a stream of

smoke rose up in a straight line I followed with my eyes until Mrs. Thorton's face was directly across from mine. Lemonade dripped off her yellow jacket, which was grayer where it was wet. Her hands were on her hips.

Chapter Fourteen

Random Bee Fact #21:
Bees' wings beat more than two hundred times per
second, creating the buzzing sound.

Candice and I sat in a room that looked like a principal's office, even though I knew there wasn't a principal of the nursing home. The books on the shelves had hard-looking leather covers like they'd never been opened. The framed paintings of birds freaked me out with their beady black eyes and sharp beaks aimed like they wanted to peck my eyes out. I stared at my hands instead, waiting for Mrs. Thorton to come out of the bathroom.

"You ruin everything," Candice whispered.

"If you weren't hovering, I wouldn't have knocked into you," I whisper-yelled back.

"No, I mean you back out of the festival, but when I say yes, you jump right back in. *And* Mrs. Thorton just let you. No one told you no. I don't even get why you wanted to join. None of this means anything to you. Some of us actually think about more than just ourselves."

"Oh, really? Because you wanted to join so badly because you cared about more than beating me?" I shook my head and let out a long, forceful breath. I was the one who could use the prize money for Dad's store. It would at least cover the cost of the desks and be one thing Dad wouldn't have to pay Naniji and Nanaji back for. But even I knew that winning wasn't going to happen even if I hadn't set the table on fire. Carissa's singing was really good. The rest of us were just time-fillers.

I looked over at Candice out of the corner of my eye. She didn't look mean anymore, her cheeks pink and a chunk of her hair pulled out of the loose braid she'd held in place from behind one ear to the other with bobby pins. But, lots of things don't look dangerous and can still hurt you. Like poison ivy or roses hiding their thorns.

"My dad's farm isn't doing well," Candice said. "The apple and peach trees didn't even blossom this spring. There aren't enough bees pollinating. Now the fall harvest is at risk, and my dad depends on sales during the fall. All that cider, the caramel apples, the pies."

Candice stared down at her blue sparkly flats.

I could understand little pieces of Candice now that I knew why she was such a know-it-all about bees. We were in similar places of wanting to help, but not really being able to do anything.

"My dad's store hasn't been doing well either."

"Oh." Candice rubbed her arms. "I didn't know."

"Yeah, my mom's . . ." I stopped from saying she was looking for jobs in New Jersey. I wasn't ready to say it out loud. "She's, well, stressed. The prize money could help pay for some stuff."

Candice twisted her skirt in her hands. "I know it's stupid, but I thought if I could be a bee ambassador and make people more aware of how important it is to save the bees, maybe I could help my dad. Maybe my parents would pay attention to me."

She says the last part quiet, but I hear it.

Now it was my turn to answer with a flat "Oh." It just kind of hung in the air, not really an answer and definitely not any help. Kind of like a cookie-scented candle—the smell is there, but no cookies. Pretty much pointless.

Candice and I both wanted to win, but our piano-recorder duet wasn't going to cut it compared to Carissa. If we wanted to win, we needed a talent that topped everyone. I knew exactly what that could be.

"Candice!" Even though my thoughts were still jumbled and all the details were nothing more than random ideas, like being in the middle of a crochet project when it looks like a mess of knots even when you know the pattern, I had a plan. I hoped that once I said it out loud, it'd sound better than it did in my head. Like maybe it'd actually sound like a good one. And be possible.

"Hmm?" Candice asked, eyeing the door of the bathroom where Mrs. Thorton was still scrubbing lemonade off her dress jacket.

I grabbed Candice's arm. "What if we do something big? Something with bees that the judges would fall off their chairs watching?"

I leaned back, opening my arms at my sides in a what-do-you-think-best-idea-ever-huh? kind of way.

Candice scrunched up her face. "Well . . . I don't know. Can we change our talent? We'll have to ask Mrs. Thorton. What are you even thinking of?"

The thing is, I had an idea for the talent, I just didn't know if Mrs. Thorton would approve. "We could cover ourselves in bees like Mr. Henry did."

"Flor, you can't just cover yourself in bees. You have to train to do that."

"Exactly. We ask Mr. Henry to teach us. We're already

at his place twice a week. We can practice with him and surprise everyone at the festival."

"I don't know, Flor. It seems risky." Candice pulled on her bottom lip.

"Come over later. We'll check the rules and if you still don't think it'll work, we'll come up with a better plan."

Mrs. Thorton came out of the bathroom, her jacket hanging over her arm. "I'm really disappointed in you girls. I expected more from you two." She took turns staring each of us down.

"Sorry," we mumbled together.

"I'm just glad no one was injured. You two must behave from now on. No more fighting."

"We promise," I said.

"Yes, Mrs. Thorton," Candice added, glancing over at me, a small smile tugging at her mouth. "We'll work together from now on."

The silence that night made it difficult to sleep. It was the kind of quiet you could hear. Like in the old Western movies Gramps used to watch. The town was deserted, windows boarded up, tumbleweeds rolling across the street just to emphasize how empty things were, but the heroes would ride into town, sitting on their horses. Listening. Waiting.

That's what it felt like. Like I was waiting for Mom and Dad to suddenly burst through a door and fight. But ever since Mom bought her ticket, it was like we were all holding our breath to see what would happen. I didn't want to think about all the ifs: if she got the job. If we moved. If Dad decided not to come with us. Wasn't that how it all started?

The quiet stretched through to morning. Fran didn't even bang my door to complain about the toothpaste glob I left in the sink last night.

I actually left the glob on purpose. Just to hear her yell, to let me know things were still "normal." Even though I hated the new normal that'd spread wider and thicker through our lives over the last year, Fran being annoyed with me was at least one thing I could usually count on.

When my bedroom door finally creaked open, I rolled over, expecting it to be Fran.

It was Mom.

"Morning, Flor."

I rolled onto my belly and turned my head to stare through the blinds that divided my window into tiny slits.

Mom sat at the end of my bed near my feet. I felt her move a stack of books and a forgotten crochet project onto the floor and waited for her to say something pointless like: "I'm doing this for us" or "I'm not trying to ruin your life" or the worst, "You have a say in this." All those things parents say but don't mean.

"I know this summer hasn't gone how you'd planned, but you've really stepped up and gone above what your dad and I asked. I'm proud of you."

Mom placed something on my back. I didn't reach for it.

"You know, Flor, Dad and I have been fighting a lot lately, but this is something we've both decided is worth me checking out. I don't even have the job yet."

The boxy feel of the package pushed into my back as Mom gave it a pat. I think she meant it to be comforting that she didn't have the job, but all I could hear ringing through my head was the "yet."

"You don't have to say anything right now, but the phone is all set up. Dad's, mine, and Naniji's numbers are all in there. Oh, and I added Brooke's, too. I'll FaceTime you from Nan's tonight. You keep helping Dad around the store, okay?"

She kissed the back of my head and closed the door behind her.

I rolled over, letting the box with my new phone hit the floor.

Part of me wanted to rip it open and send messages to Brooke and set a cool wallpaper and finally get some apps

I'd been dying to try, but a much bigger part of me didn't want anything to do with the Bribe Phone no matter how good it would finally feel to slide it into my back pocket.

I stood up, letting my comforter fall onto it, burying it.

Chapter Fifteen

Random Bee Fact #23:
The stinger from a bee will continue to pump venom into your body even after the bee has died.

Mom was too happy to hear I'd invited Candice over.

The last time Candice had been to my house was in third grade a few months after the festival. We were having a sleepover and as we brushed our teeth just before going to bed she turned to me and said, "My mom told me I should be glad I didn't win Little Miss Honeybee because people who are pretty as kids turn out to be ugly when they grow up."

I'd started to cry. I couldn't picture Mrs. Holloway saying something like that, but hearing Candice say it made me want to throw up toothpaste. Faking a tummy ache wasn't too difficult. Mom called Candice's mom and she came to pick her up. We never had another sleepover after that.

Candice hadn't always been horrible. In fact, on the first day of kindergarten when Steven asked me what language I spoke, she'd squirmed between us in the circle and whispered something to him. I still remembered sucking in my stomach, prepared for the teasing, but she turned back to me with a huge grin and said, "Want to play at recess?" Later she told me Steven played at her house after school sometimes and he hid behind the couch whenever the Count came on *Sesame Street*.

Remembering Kindergarten Candice, who was my friend, mixed with Third-to-Sixth-Grade Candice, who was my enemy, and adding Right-Now Candice, who just wanted to help her parents, was like trying to piece a broken eggshell back together. There were too many little pieces, making it impossible to make sense of.

I thought I was ready for this, having her in my house again, but I fixed my hair three different ways before settling on a messy side braid and I even took off my crocheted choker only to put it back on just before she knocked on the door. It wasn't that I cared how I looked, more that I needed to keep my hands busy.

"Morning, Candice," Mom said, opening the door and waving me closer with the arm still hidden behind the door. "Come in. Have you had breakfast?"

"Yes, thanks," Candice said, walking through the door. She looked around, her eyes darting here and there. Aside from adding fresh flowers from the garden in the summer or updated school photos, my house looked exactly like it had since kindergarten. I thought of myself like my house—pretty much staying the same, just everything else around me becoming different. But, right then, with Candice standing in my house, I knew something deep inside of me had changed from third grade. Kind of like a peach that looks fresh and ripe on the outside, but when you cut it open it's rotten just around the pit. On the outside, walking away from our friendship had been a good thing. I'd met Brooke, but it'd also left a mark on me inside. It made me feel things in bold print. Things like **anger** and **hate** where before had only been annoyance and dislike.

"I'm so glad you two are doing this pageant together this summer," Mom said, bringing me out of my thoughts. "Otherwise with Brooke away at band camp, Flor would be moping around wasting all her time." She pulled me into a sideways hug, dragging me into the conversation.

"I'm off to class soon, but Fran will be here till ten and

I'll come back by lunch." The entire time Mom talked she led Candice into the kitchen and poured her a glass of pomegranate juice.

"Your mom must be swamped at the café with the tourists this summer," Mom said.

"Mm-hmm." Candice swallowed down the juice with a look I couldn't quite read. Maybe the juice was too sour or maybe Mom's chatter made her as uncomfortable as it made me.

I grabbed one of the granola bars Fran had made and left in a container on the counter and shoved it into my mouth for an excuse to not have to talk.

Mom raised her eyebrows at me. Code for: *Don't be rude. Offer one to your guest.* It wasn't like I was hoarding gooey, homemade brownies. It was a Fran experiment, but if Mom insisted.

"Would you like one? Fran made them. So beware," I said, spraying pumpkin and chia seeds down the front of my shirt. "The taste is fine, it's the chewing that's a problem."

Candice snorted and reached for one.

I had almost forgotten she could laugh.

Mom twisted on the cap of her travel mug, smiling at Candice and me like she'd created world peace. "See you girls later."

Once Mom closed the door, there was nothing to fill the awkward silence that seeped into the room. The sound of us chewing Fran's granola bars seemed to echo. I tried to imagine that Brooke was sitting there and what I'd say to her, but that was just the thing—if Brooke were sitting there I wouldn't *have* to think about what to say, I'd just say it. Candice and I hadn't had that level of conversation in years unless it was to trade insults.

"Fran's still experimenting," Candice said, holding up her granola bar with a bite taken out.

"She hasn't gotten much better. Obviously," I said, still chewing.

Candice laughed. "Remember the blueberry muffins?"

I remembered, but was surprised Candice did. When Fran had first started baking in sixth grade, she put liquid soap in the muffin batter instead of oil because Mom used similar fancy bottles with spouts for both. I caught myself just before I let a laugh bubble out at the memory.

"You don't have to finish that if you don't want to," I said, nodding at the granola bar.

Candice shrugged. "It's not too bad, just superhard to chew."

"I guess we can start our research? I'll use my mom's laptop and you can use the desktop."

We moved to the small room off the kitchen that Mom

used as an office. Candice pulled a purple binder out of her bag and some highlighters.

"Ready to figure out how to cover ourselves in bees?" I asked.

"First of all, you've got to call it 'bee bearding,' Flor. I watched a few videos last night and it's better if we train to cover parts of your face and not your entire body. It would take several frames of bees to cover your body and could take up to fifteen or twenty minutes. Our talents are only given three minutes each, including setup and cleanup." She pulled out the rules.

I grabbed the paper from her. She was right. We weren't going to have a lot of time and we needed to make a big impression if we wanted to be better than Carissa.

"Here, I'll show you what I'm talking about." Candice typed "How to bee beard" into the YouTube search function. We clicked through several videos, but the best we found were by an old guy who taught a group of people how to bee beard in just one sitting.

Candice scribbled down some key points like weather conditions and feeding the bees sugar water while I focused on making a list of supplies we'd need. I wasn't quite as prepared (or at all prepared) like Candice with her binder and color-coordinated dividers, so I grabbed a piece of paper near the printer. Thankfully it was Fran's reject stack of recipes she'd been compiling for the food pantry. "Kale Hash in a Dash" had been a dud since kale didn't come in a can, so I turned it over and listed out all the stuff we'd need: cotton balls to stuff up our nose and in our ears. Vaseline to put near our eyes and cheeks so the bees would stay closer to our chins and look more like a beard than a face mob.

Candice flipped through the yellow section of her binder, where she'd put the forms Mrs. Thorton had passed out. "I was thinking that you could do the bee beard while I do a speech."

Before I could argue that I thought we were both going to have bees on us, she flipped to a blue section of her binder.

"I've been collecting lots of bee facts over the past few years, and I think it's important that the crowd sees the bees as harmless and helpful."

"I just thought we were doing this together," I said, not sure why I was suddenly so nervous. I squirmed in my chair, thinking about the videos I'd just watched of bees crawling around on people's faces. I knew this was all my idea, but it felt safer to do something like this with someone else. Like whenever I rode a roller coaster, I felt better just knowing there were other people on the ride, like my chances of getting hurt were somehow less if there were other people doing the same thing.

"Well, look here. This video is of two guys who've never done a bee beard before. Ever." We watched as the first guy tied the queen cage (a plastic kind of holder the beekeeper slipped the queen into) under his chin like a helmet strap, and the bees from the hive slowly settled on his face, surrounding the queen and forming a thrumming beard of bees. He stood up and jumped, letting the bees fall exactly how Mr. Henry had. His friend took the queen cage and did the same thing, but the beekeeper took out a leaf blower and swept the beard away after they'd all settled. The second guy got stung once.

"See?" Candice said. "It's not really that bad."

If I had to choose which was worse, moving to New Jersey or getting stung a few times, I guess I would choose risking getting stung.

Chapter Sixteen

Random Bee Fact #56:
Bees are picky eaters. They start with their favorite
flowers and save their least favorite for last.

It was six thirty in the evening and still bright outside. One of my favorite things about summer—nights that feel like daytime. Mom kissed my head good-bye and hugged me. It felt good to have the softer version of her instead of the pointy, jabby one, but I didn't let myself relax into her hug too much. She *was* off to New Jersey.

"Fran will be home soon. There are leftovers in the fridge or you can wait for her and eat whatever she makes. While you're waiting, clean up your room," Mom called as Dad pulled her luggage out the door to the car. "Love you." It's funny because Mom always lists off things to do as a farewell and I really do think it means she loved us.

I waved and stood at the door until they were out of the driveway.

I'd been avoiding Mom as much as possible for the past few weeks and now that she was gone, it felt like I had nothing else to do. I crashed on my bed, digging the Bribe Phone out from under my comforter, then set it in front of me.

I hadn't messaged Brooke back in more than two weeks. She called Mom's phone when I was at the food pantry once, but when I called her back it went straight to her messages.

Mom had charged the phone. It wasn't *new*-new; it was Dad's old one.

I didn't even have to scroll to find Brooke's number, since there were only a few numbers programmed in. Instead of messaging Brooke right away—mostly because I couldn't figure out where to begin with telling her everything that'd been happening—I chose a cool wallpaper and set up my password. Then I opened up the messaging app and typed and deleted a few messages before settling on something true, holding back all the details I wasn't ready to put into words.

Got my own phone!!!!!

So much to catch up on.

Can't wait to see you soon!

Miss you. xoxo

Brooke messaged back:

Haven't heard from you in forever!

Miss you so much. 2 more weeks girl!

I fell back against my pillows. It felt good to know that Brooke wasn't mad at me for not sending her any messages for weeks, but also made me feel guiltier for not telling her what was going on. Like how Mom just left for New Jersey or how I kind of maybe understood Candice better and could possibly find her a little bit nice and funny and could even think of her as a friend.

I'd always told Brooke everything. We even got dressed in the same changing rooms when we bought new bathing suits and school clothes.

But maybe Candice and I could pull off the bee beard and win. Brooke would be back from camp before the festival. She'd watch us win with our amazing talent and there'd be no New Jersey to not tell her about because I wouldn't be moving after all.

Friday morning, I spent extra time brushing my teeth and trying to come up with a way to ask Mr. Henry about the bees. I tied my hair back into a loose bun and mouthed the words to the script Candice had written out for me. We'd gone back and forth on how to ask him. I thought a more straightforward approach would be best. Dad liked to say, "Hard sells need a hard push." Candice said I'd just scare Mr. Henry off.

Fran was waiting for me in the kitchen when I finally came out. "Hurry up, Flor. I'm going to be late for work."

"Just a minute. I need to grab some breakfast."

"You should have done that ten minutes ago. I'm waiting for two and you better be in the car."

I grabbed a slice of bread, smothered it with peanut butter, and ran after Fran before she could slam the door in my face. We pulled in front of Aunt Bee's Café a few minutes later. Candice was waiting outside by a parking meter. She held up the binder before setting it on her lap as she got into the car.

Candice and I had everything we needed to bee beard, except for one thing.

The bees.

Mr. Henry sat in his wheelchair on the porch with the local paper spread out across his lap. His beard looked like Dad's after a long weekend of not shaving—scattered patches of black and gray, making his face look dirty. He tapped the side of his wheelchair with a cane and his eyes followed us from the car to where he was sitting at the bottom of the ramp that led to the side door of his house.

"I'll be back at twelve." Fran drove off, barely waiting for us to close the car door.

Mr. Henry tapped his fingers on a cane he had propped against his leg. "That fence is ready for a second coat." He nodded toward the fence past the barn that lined his property. Candice and I had spent the past two weeks adding a fresh coat of white paint to it.

"Oh. Um." I stuffed my hands into my back pockets, but could hear Dad say, "Confidence is the first rule of sales," in my head. I pulled my hands out of my pockets and stood up straight. I tried to force out the words Candice had told me, but Mr. Henry's gaze was like that Hole in the Wall game where you had to squeeze your body through almost impossible shapes. The way he squinted his eyes at me when I spoke, it was like he could warp my thoughts into words I hadn't meant to say. "We'd like you to train us to bee beard for our talent for the festival."

Candice cleared her throat beside me, hugging the binder to her chest.

"Mmm." An angry hum of a sound came out of his unmoving mouth.

Mr. Henry grabbed the cane he'd been tapping against his wheelchair and jabbed it in the grass with a thud. Slowly he pushed himself up. I never realized just how tall he was. The times I'd seen him out of his chair, he was still crouched or leaning. He looked at Candice and then back at me. Each second felt like minutes. I didn't dare breathe out of my mouth. I just let little trickles of air seep in and out of my nose.

"You two think you can bee beard."

It wasn't a question.

If it weren't for Dad's store, I might have backed off. But, after watching the videos of people letting the bees attach themselves to their face and hardly a single one getting stung, it didn't seem like such an impossible thing.

"We've done some research. See?" Candice held our binder full of lists and rules and supplies.

Mr. Henry raised his eyebrows as he flipped through the notes Candice had organized.

"And we've asked our parents and have permission from Mrs. Thorton," I added, hoping to skip over any questions he might have about wanting to call our parents.

Candice shook her head like maybe I'd been too obvious, but Mr. Henry just rubbed the stubble along his jaw, making the same sound as Fran scraping nutmeg on her Microplane. A rough *scritch-scratch* was the only sound as he flipped through the pages of the binder.

"You've obviously put a lot of thought into this," Mr. Henry said, closing the binder.

I knew that look on his face. The eyebrows slanted

down, lips sucked in. It's the same look couples got in the store when one of them wanted to buy the bed, but the other one wasn't so sure. It wasn't a definite no, but wasn't a definite yes, either.

He pushed the binder back toward Candice. "Follow me. Let's see if you can put your money where your mouth is."

I swallowed hard. It felt like my throat was already lined with squirming bees as I shuffled behind Candice and Mr. Henry toward the barn. Candice turned and flashed me a thumbs-up and a toothy smile, but I could barely manage to keep my feet moving. I thought the *sale* would be the difficult part, it hadn't really, really hit me yet what it'd be like letting a hive of bees flash-mob my face.

Chapter Seventeen

Random Bee Fact #71:
Ruan Liangming holds the Guinness World Record for having 637,000 bees on his body. That's 636,999 more than I'd ever had on me.

My feet moved in slow motion behind Mr. Henry as he pushed his wheelchair along the plywood planks he'd laid from the edge of the paved driveway out to the barn. "Grab that hive tool, a lighter, and the smoker from the drawer," he said to me.

He turned to Candice. "You know what a queen cage looks like?"

"Yes, sir."

"Grab that, too."

I scurried after Candice to get the netted hats while she colleced other things.

Thankfully, all these things weren't so strange to me now that we'd spent hours watching videos about it. Candice held up the queen cage, a small plastic netted thing with straps on either side. We needed to remove the queen bee from the hive and put her in the queen cage, which would go around my neck in order to attract the other bees to me, since the bees' instinct was to hover around and protect their queen wherever she went.

From the outside, the hives were these simple, clean-looking white boxes, but I knew now that inside was an ever-moving cluster of bees.

"This hive." Mr. Henry tapped the white box in front of him lightly with his cane. A few bees lingering near the hole at the side inspected his cane before going back inside the hive. I wondered if they went back in to report to the queen what was going on. Did bees even have words for "cane" or "humans"?

"We'll pull out each frame and find the queen," he said. "They've been a robust hive since I got them a few years back. They're the ones I trust the most."

Mr. Henry gestured for Candice and me to slip the netted hats on over our heads, but he stayed bare-handed and faced as he pointed at the hive tool I was squeezing too tightly.

"You remember what to do?" he asked.

I nodded and pulled out the frame at the far left, holding it up so Mr. Henry could use his Tin Man oilcan thing to puff smoke toward the bees a few times.

Candice leaned in close and didn't shy away from putting her finger right into each frame just like Mr. Henry had when we'd helped him inspect the hives before.

We each scanned the frame, turning it over slowly, looking for the queen. I knew from the videos we'd watched and the facts Candice had rattled off that she'd be almost twice as big as the other bees and have a colored dot on her back.

With the constant motion of the bees, trying to focus on one individually was like trying to follow a piece of popcorn in one of those massive popcorn poppers at the movie theater. The bees piled on top of one another, some getting buried, some crawling away, some flying off to land on different spots, all getting churned around, making it impossible to figure out if it was a new bee or a bee I'd already seen.

The queen wasn't in the first three frames we pulled out. Finally, in the next frame Candice found her. "Here. Got her," Candice whispered, and kept her finger in front of the queen. The queen crawled slowly around the frame as the other bees bumbled about.

Mr. Henry smoked the frame before he reached toward her. The bees seemed to trust him. Even when he grabbed for the queen, she didn't put up a fight. He just scooped her up gently with his thumb and pointer finger. Candice passed him the queen cage and in one quick movement she was inside.

"Wow. How'd you learn to do all this?" I asked.

Mr. Henry shrugged. "Used to be a passion of mine. Was researching apitherapy."

"Oh, I read about that," Candice butted in. "Bee venom and honey can be used to cure all kinds of things."

Mr. Henry nodded and then motioned to me. "Don't put that frame back in. We'll test out bee bearding with a single frame. There're enough bees on one frame to create a beard. Let's see how you girls handle it."

"Actually, how Florence handles it," Candice said.

"Oh, I see." Mr. Henry nodded at me. There was a seriousness to his face for just a moment. Like maybe he was surprised it was me and not Candice.

The constant movement of the bees made my fingers tingle like they were falling asleep. The frame was getting heavy after holding it for just a few minutes. "About how many bees are there on the frame?" I asked.

"Ten to twelve thousand. We'll take the queen cage off when about a hundred or so land on you. That'll be a good first try, and only because you've got someone around who knows what they're doing."

I wanted to gulp, but I couldn't get enough spit in my mouth. I blinked my eyes a few times instead. A *hundred* bees.

On. My. Face.

Mr. Henry stood up from his wheelchair, leaning heavily on his cane and resting against the hive next to the one we'd taken the queen out of. "Take a seat." He motioned toward his wheelchair for me to sit down.

"Are you okay to stand?" I asked.

"Of course, of course." He waved his hand at my question and shooed at Candice. "Tie the queen cage on her arm. Florence, keep your bee hat on. We'll just do a test run around your arm."

I sat as still as I could manage while Candice tied the queen cage above my elbow. Even though having bees crawl all over my face had been my idea, I was relieved to practice on my arm first.

"Is that okay?" Candice asked. I thought she was asking Mr. Henry until I realized they were quiet because they were waiting for me to answer. I nodded.

The hum in the air from the bees grew louder to the

point I could feel it vibrate through my chest and arms, making her words one long buzz mixed in with the bees.

Mr. Henry showed Candice how to hold the single frame just above my lap and give it a gentle shake to loosen the bees. They hadn't yet noticed their queen wasn't with them.

A tiny cluster of three bees fumbled up my arm to the queen cage. Each time they hit my arm or each other, they let out a zap more than a buzz. Slowly, more and more bees peeled away from the frame, uncovering a greater number underneath. Twelve thousand bees suddenly looked like twelve million.

The tickle of bee legs ran up and down my arm. As the bees clung to me, the hum of their wings and the constant buzz of their bodies relaxed me, and my breaths started to become a natural, slow up-and-down without me even having to focus on it.

Their tiny weightless legs weighed down on my arm, becoming scratchy and heavy, feeling way more like the fake plastic spiders we put in the fake cobwebs at Dad's store for Halloween.

Mr. Henry nodded at my arm. "When you're ready, stand up and give your arm a good shake. They'll fall right off." He gave his arm a quick fling to show me how.

Candice stepped closer to me and held the frame out

flat like a lunch tray. I held my breath and flung my arm toward it, waiting for the burning feeling of stings, but they never came. All but a few bees fell right off of me like shaking sand off a beach towel. Mr. Henry reached over and untied the queen cage from my elbow, which was all that the lingering bees needed to move on. I released a huge lungful of air. I'd read so many times of people holding their breath without meaning to in books, but this was the first time I'd actually experienced it in real life.

In a way, having that many bees on me had been no big deal now that it was over, but, at the same time, it had also been a huge deal.

Candice bounced up and down, a grin spread across her face. I was so relieved it'd actually worked, I had to pull my arms behind my back to keep from throwing them around her in a hug. The realization of what I'd done—had a hundred bees on my arm without being stung once—left me almost floating, like an insect in the middle of amber.

Chapter Eighteen

Random Bee Fact #13:
Two tablespoons of honey would fuel a bee's flight
around the world.

As Fran was driving us back to town, Candice asked if I wanted to have lunch at her mom's café.

"Um. Yeah." Of course I did. I hadn't eaten there since Brooke left for camp, plus I could grab a honey bun for Dad.

"Fran, do you want to join us?" Candice asked.

"No, thanks. I've got stuff to do." Fran used her nice voice, then turned to me and used her big-sister voice: "You'll have to walk down to the store when you're done. I have to stop by work to pick up my paycheck at the pool."

Candice took me through the alley door and I followed

her past the dishwashers and right to the three massive refrigerators lined up on a wall.

"I hope you don't mind, but my mom only lets me use the cold cuts to make a sandwich for lunch."

"Sounds good to me." I pretty much followed Candice around the kitchen as she gathered the honey shaved ham, honey mustard sauce, lettuce, tomato slices, and plates.

"My mom says the secret to a good sandwich is sauce." Candice used a spatula to wipe the honey mustard on both slices of bread for each of our sandwiches.

"My dad's always giving me tips, too. But for selling things."

"My mom has a never-ending list of them." Candice layered the sandwiches and we grabbed an open bag of chips and dumped a bunch on both our plates. "Let's see if there's an open table."

A small table near the bathrooms was open, so Candice and I sat down.

"We should make a detailed list of everything we need for bee bearding and a schedule," Candice said.

"I thought we did already at my house."

"That was just getting the rules and stuff together so we could convince Mr. Henry. We've got to time my speech with your bees. Do you have cotton balls and Vaseline at home?"

I nodded, because I'd just shoved a huge bite of sandwich into my mouth.

"Good, because once we practice with the bees on your face, we'll need to cover most of it in Vaseline so the bees only settle around your chin where there's none. Plus, we've got to figure out how Mr. Henry's going to get the bees to the festival and how we're going to keep it all a surprise."

"Surprise" maybe wasn't the right word. The rules didn't state we couldn't bee beard, but we also hadn't asked Mrs. Thorton about it, either.

"Well, if it isn't just the sweetest thing seeing two of my honeybees working together just like you promised!" Mrs. Thorton walked right up to our table from the direction of the bathroom. Her loud voice drew looks from the other customers.

I forced my face into a smile; the honey mustard on my sandwich burned down my throat as I swallowed. Candice coughed into her napkin.

"Yep," Candice said, recovering enough to speak. "Just working together. Like we promised."

I fake-laughed along with Mrs. Thorton.

"Actually, Mrs. Thorton," Candice said, "we were just talking about our talent and . . ." She paused to clear her throat.

I tried to kick her under the table, but stubbed my toe on the table leg instead. She couldn't ask Mrs. Thorton, not now that Mr. Henry had agreed. What if she said no?

"We've been working so well together since the . . ." Candice made some exaggerated motions with her hands like she was re-creating the fire from the nursing home.

"Incident?" Mrs. Thorton offered, raising her eyebrows.

"Yes, since then. Well, we were wondering if we could—"

"What she's trying to ask is can we create a movie to be projected behind us?" I asked, avoiding looking at Candice. I had to cut her off before she exposed our bee-beard idea.

"Well, Carissa has one, so I'd suggest you create something different from hers," Mrs. Thorton said.

"It will *definitely* be different from Carissa's," Candice said.

"Just be sure you get the video to us in advance. We'll need it approved and I have to be sure the tech team can get it all set up with the doohickies."

"Oh, great. Thank you, Mrs. Thorton," I said. "I guess we'd better hurry up and finish our lunch so we can get that video completed." I coughed to cover up Candice's foot hitting my leg.

"Of course. Enjoy, girls."

Candice smiled and waved until Mrs. Thorton was out of earshot. "You are so obvious."

"I was saving us."

"Did you really think I was going to tell her about the bee beard? I'm not stupid, Flor."

I clenched my teeth together, feeling that all-too-familiar sharpness of her words, and prepared to defend myself, when Candice started to giggle. Then it turned into one of those silent laughs where her entire body was shaking, but no noise came out. I couldn't help it, I started to laugh too.

"What's so funny?" I asked between laughs.

"She was like, 'The tech team needs to set up the doohickies.'" She grabbed her stomach and I relaxed into a real laugh.

Candice's mom spotted us and walked over. "Hey, girls. How's the sandwich, Florence?"

"It's great. Thanks."

"The secret to a good sandwich is the sauce," Mrs. Holloway said with a wink as she walked back to the counter to take another lunch order.

"I told you," Candice said, starting another fit of laughter between us.

We'd been together every other day for a month, but we hadn't once been *this* chummy. As I laughed, a sense of weirdness twisted inside me like a dirty dishrag dripping bits and drops of about every emotion it could have swiped up. Surprise that maybe we were more than frenemies. Worry that I was betraying Brooke in some way. A hint of relief. Like maybe things were really behind us and we could be actual friends. Which also made me feel nervous, like this all teetered on the edge of a cliff and could end with one small push.

Chapter Nineteen

Random Bee Fact #112:
Bees have no eyelids, so they can't close their eyes to sleep;
they simply stop moving when they need to rest.

C andice's mom sent me off with a bag of honey buns. I held them up in front of Dad when I got back to the store.

"Ah, champ! Good thing you brought snacks. Go look out back."

Dad took the bag and grabbed a honey bun as he followed me through the door into the break room.

"Go on, all the way out," Dad said through a bite.

The back door was wedged open a crack with a doorstop. I pulled it all the way open to find about twenty different sized and shaped boxes, filling his usual parking space. I instantly thought back to the mattress costume and how Mom had reacted. Thankfully she was all the way in New Jersey and we had five days to deal with this if it was another costume gone wrong.

"Dad, what is it?" Even as I asked, I wasn't sure I wanted to know the answer.

"Well, your mom and I came to a compromise. She went to New Jersey, we got the desks. It was a great idea, kiddo. Your mom agreed it was worth the try to see if desks would boost sales."

I didn't know what to say. Seeing another idea of mine fall into place felt like I was one of those heroic characters in a movie and things were finally going my way.

Dad held the bag out to me. "Eat up, we've got a lot of work to do."

We finished our honey buns and carried the desks inside. It took us a few hours to put together the five desks Mom and Dad had agreed on.

"Let's leave these where they are for now," Dad said after tightening the last screw on a light brown wooden desk that matched one of the bunk-bed sets perfectly. "I've got to run to the hardware store to get some wall fasteners and scuff pads, and we can figure out where we want things to go tomorrow."

Dad dropped me off at home on his way to the hardware store. "I won't be long but start dinner without me."

I was sure I was dreaming when the smell of fried chicken hit me as I walked into the kitchen. A platter of chicken wings and a bowl of mashed potatoes with a little pitcher of gravy sat on the counter. "Fran?" I yelled. She didn't answer and my stomach let out a long, low growl. I decided Fran must be in the shower, so I dug in.

The chicken wings were actually cauliflower disguised as chicken. Maybe I'd eaten one too many of her experiments, but the wings actually tasted good. I polished off three scoops of mashed potatoes and gravy and scooped out another bowl to take in front of the television.

Fran was on the couch. No television on. No radio on. No sense that she even knew I was staring at her.

"Are you okay?" I asked.

Her eyes flickered in my direction, but they didn't focus on anything.

"Did you forget to drink water, and have sunstroke?" I asked. Because that happened to Brooke last summer and her eyes had looked just like that—all faraway and glassy.

"No. Idiot," Fran said mostly into the couch pillow.

"I'm not an idiot," I said, rolling my eyes. "Don't mope in the middle of the house and make fake fried chicken if you don't want people to know what's wrong with you." I grabbed the remote and squeezed at the edge of the couch so I didn't accidentally touch her.

"Leave me alone," she mumbled.

"I'm not even touching you. If you wanted me to stay out of your business you should've made spinach wraps filled with pesto ricotta something or other."

"That doesn't even make culinary sense." Fran squeezed the throw pillow closer to her as she rolled her eyes at me.

"You don't make human conversation sense."

This was going nowhere. I clicked on the television and scrolled through some options before choosing to rewatch a series I'd already finished so I didn't have to pay too much attention. When I finished the last bite, I licked the side of the bowl, where there was still a streak of potatoes, and set the bowl down on the coffee table.

I closed my eyes and thought about real fried chicken and how Mom was gone for a few days and I could probably talk Dad into us getting a bucket of chicken one night. Then out of nowhere Fran started talking. I kept my eyes closed just in case it was only because she thought I was sleeping and not listening to her.

"Boys are a pain. Don't ever like one. Don't ever talk to one. Don't even look at them. You think they're cute, but really all they do is laugh like donkeys and do things like fart and burp with their friends. Once you see them do that, suddenly they don't look so cute anymore."

Duh. We did have a dad. I could have told her that. Dad liked to walk around in his underwear after his shower and he farted down the hallway. I mean, come on, I couldn't believe that for my entire life he really thought we couldn't hear it when he farted. Obviously, we all know boys are gross.

"So why is kissing such a big deal?" It was a good question when I really thought about it. The way boys shoved food into their mouths at school. The shine of grease around their mouths and how they wiped at their faces and noses like they didn't care that napkins had been invented for a reason. Like I'd want to kiss *that*.

"Well, usually the boy lays off the grossness for a few days and you think he might be becoming civilized and maybe a kiss would be nice. And it is. At first. If he's any good at it."

"How many boys have you kissed?"

"Two."

"Two?"

"Tom Brennen last summer and Josh Freeman last week. We've been hanging out this summer at work."

"How did it happen?" How *did* these things happen?

"What do you mean, how did it happen? Hanging out after work. Talking, eating ice cream—"

"Did you still have ice cream in your mouth?"

"Don't be so stupid, Flo. You don't kiss with food in your mouth."

"Well, I know *that*." Actually, I didn't. I had no idea what or how to do anything boy-related. I could hardly talk to them anymore. For the longest time they were just other people in my class, but this year at school they'd become . . . different. If I couldn't talk to them, how in the world would I be able to kiss them? Did you push his face away and finish your food first? I mean, I'd probably need to take a drink of something before I'd be ready for a kiss.

Swallow my food, take a drink of water, push my hair off my face, lick my lips, and then be ready. How did anyone ever have time to kiss if it took so much preparation?

"Don't worry about it. You shouldn't do it and I wish I never had." Fran squeezed her eyes closed like she could get rid of the kiss that way.

"Really?" I always imagined that everything that happened to Fran was movie-perfect. I couldn't understand why she wished she'd never kissed a boy. It might never happen to me, and I wanted to know everything.

"Because. Boys are stupid. I told Josh that Mom was going for the job interview and that we might be moving, just letting him know what was going on. I thought he cared. Next thing I knew, he was kissing *Carissa Williams* in the first-aid station."

"Eww, near all the CPR dummies? Creepy."

"Focus, Flor. That's not the point; the point is my life is over. I hope Mom gets the job. I'll be glad to get dragged off to New Jersey."

"What do you mean? You want to go? It's not even for sure yet."

"It might as well be. Don't you know how these interviews go? They wouldn't have her fly there if it wasn't serious."

Is that how it worked? Even if that was true, I couldn't believe Fran was suddenly okay with moving. Just a few nights ago she'd been so upset with Mom for making the plans and not asking what we wanted. Stupid boys.

"I hate to break it to you, but if Mom gets that job, we'll all be moving." Fran scooted up to a sitting position.

That's because Fran didn't know there was still a way we could stay. If she did, she wouldn't be giving up over some boy. We had the desks, and Candice and I had a real chance at winning with the bee beard.

Chapter Twenty

Random Bee Fact #95:
Honey stored in an airtight container never spoils. Three-thousand-year-old jars of honey from Egyptian tombs have been found perfectly preserved.

It was easier to feel sorry for Fran when she was moping on the couch and making halfway normal food, but she had gone from mopey to full-on monster mode by the next morning. Her puffy eyes were the only sign she'd been upset the night before.

"Did you make your bed?" she asked as I came out of my room, stuffing Vaseline and cotton balls into my backpack.

Just because she was a neat freak, she thought I should be one too. I tried to close my door behind me, but Fran put her hand on the door and pushed it open. "I don't believe it. Mom said to clean your room."

"I'll do it after I go to Mr. Henry's."

"Do it now." Fran turned and walked down the hall toward the kitchen. "And brush your teeth. Your breath smells like a moldy life jacket."

In the car on the way to pick up Candice, Fran tried to hide her puffy eyes under a pair of sunglasses. She kept the music loud and didn't even bother to say hi when Candice got into the car. We had barely scrambled out of the backseat at the top of Mr. Henry's driveway before she screeched away.

"What's her deal?" Candice asked.

"Josh, her maybe-kind-of boyfriend, kissed Carissa in the CPR room and she thinks her life is over. Not only that, now she actually wants my mom to get this stupid job in New Jersey so we'll move and she won't have to see him ever again." Everything spilled out like the watery stuff in a mustard bottle right when you open the cap.

"Wait a minute. What? Your mom is getting a new job? You're moving?"

Candice leaned forward. Her eyes might have been watery.

Her shock reminded me that even though I'd told her the store wasn't doing well, I hadn't mentioned Mom's job out loud to anyone except to my family.

I'm not sure what surprised me the most, Candice's reaction or how I'd let it all slip to her without having told Brooke any of it. Candice and I had only just started interacting in this weird space between hating each other and not hating each other, which wasn't exactly spill-your-guts-friendship zone. Yet there I was, gushing the details of Fran's breakup and my family's maybe move. The whole thing felt like laundry hanging outside on a clothesline. It might be clean, but there were bras and underwear right out there with shirts and pants for anyone to see.

"Wow, that sucks. What did Brooke say?"

"Well, I haven't told her."

Candice's mouth fell open, but she quickly closed it. "Oh."

"I was going to, but I kind of keep thinking there's still a chance it won't happen, so what's the point? Fran said it's stupid to keep hoping my mom will change her mind if we win."

"Win the festival? How's that going to help?"

"The money. I came up with a plan to buy some desks to help my dad expand the business. I want to use the money to pay him back or order more if we sell enough." Even saying it out loud started to sound as stupid as Fran had made me feel when we'd fought about it.

The door of Mr. Henry's house slammed closed and

the now-familiar *whap* of plywood hitting the steps with the whir of wheels followed. "Grab the queen cage and the supplies I left on the worktable," he said, rolling himself toward the hives.

We filled our arms with the smoker, a lighter, and some newspaper, along with the netted hats.

The low hum of the bees calmed me as we got closer to where Mr. Henry was sitting among the hives. I never would have thought that sitting in the middle of hundreds of thousands of bees would be relaxing, but the dull buzzing was weirdly like the whir of a fan.

"We're going to take your practicing up a step," Mr. Henry said. "You need to get a feel for the process before we get the bees to land on your face. So I think we should put Vaseline on your arm, leaving just your forearm exposed. But let's get the queen out first."

Candice and I slipped on our hats and this time worked together taking out the frames before finding the queen. Mr. Henry clicked the queen cage closed around her as Candice helped me spread Vaseline on my left arm. It felt like melted wax on my skin. Bees flew around us, bumping into the netting on the hats and landing on our shirts just long enough to touch us before flying away.

Candice tied the queen cage just below my elbow and I held my arm out like I was putting it in a blood pressure cuff.

"Now be still and I'll hold the frame close to you." Mr. Henry rolled his chair with one hand, holding the frame out with the other.

Probably because Mr. Henry had said "Be still" behind and inside my ear, even weird parts at the back of my head suddenly felt itchy. All these places I usually forgot about were suddenly screaming at me to scratch them.

"Okay. I'm going to bring the frame close to you. Looks like a lot, but I'll pull them away once a couple hundred land on you."

I nodded in small, slow movements.

Mr. Henry sat in front of me, holding the frame in the same up-and-down position it had been inside the hive. The bees didn't bother with me. They hovered around the frame and didn't seem to notice I was there with their queen on my arm. A few bees did their clumsy bump into my arm, quickly escaping the Vaseline. Finally a few found the queen. Once they did, the others followed. About ten bees dotted my arm, landing, hopping off, landing again. Each time closer to the queen. Ten became twenty and then I lost count. The bees crowded the outside of the queen cage at first, then they spread down my arm. The bottom layer crawled and buzzed; the top layer pushed and crowded against one another. My forearm tingled with the movement. They really did stay away from the Vaseline.

"You're doing great," Mr. Henry said. His voice was low and calm. "They must be getting heavy. When you're ready, hold your arm out straight and give it a good fling. Candice, you'll need to take the queen cage off and put it over here near the hive. The bees will follow her."

Candice nodded and I swallowed.

Taking a deep breath, I took my time straightening my arm out, holding it in front of me. Then I lifted it up next to my ear before swinging it down in a quick chop. A cluster of bees fell from my arm, still clinging to one another before flying in all directions.

Candice untied the queen cage and put it on top of the hive. Several bees hovered around my arm and I somehow managed to stay calm until they realized the queen wasn't there anymore and flew away.

"That was good," Mr. Henry said. "Real good."

"Flor, that was great," Candice said, squeezing my hand, bring feeling back to my arm.

"Thanks," I said as I let out a breath.

"That's enough for today." Mr. Henry opened the queen cage and held it over the frame until she lazily emerged. The other bees filled in around her until she disappeared.

Candice and I helped put the two lids back onto the hive before collecting the tools we'd used.

As we made our way back to the barn, Mr. Henry said, "Mrs. Thorton asked if I'd donate my cars for the afternoon of the festival. Was thinking you girls could choose the one you want to ride in first."

"Really?" Candice asked. "Flor, it'll be just like when your grandpa let us ride on his!"

"Go on. Through that door you can push the button and open all the garage doors."

Candice did, and all five garage doors creaked and groaned open. Behind each door was a gleaming car. A dark green car with white interior and a cream convertible cover. A tiny red sports car you could tell was old by the big wheels and long hood. A sky-blue car so wide I wondered how it fit in a single lane on the road. A silvery white car with a back and front so long it touched the back wall of the garage to fit inside. But it was the banana-yellow convertible with the butter-colored interior that caught my eye.

Mr. Henry noticed and rolled over to it. "She's gorgeous. The first one I restored."

Gramps would have known every detail down to the exact engine parts. I'd spent many Sundays with him in his garage, but I never could remember anything about car engines or how they worked, only that my favorite was the baby-blue convertible with hand-cranked windshield wipers that we'd ridden in for the festival in third grade.

Candice bounced over to the yellow car. "Oh, this is perfect. What do you think, Flor?"

I nodded, my face smiling.

I started to feel the excitement of the festival I hadn't felt since third grade.

Chapter Twenty-One

Random Bee Fact #108:
Bees produce sixty to one hundred pounds of honey a
year, two to three times more than they need.

Fran took Candice and me to Mr. Henry's again at the end of the week. We'd spent the day before at the food pantry taste-testing her new recipes. Chickpea and spinach soup (definitely could have used more salt). Tuna and white bean patties (could have used fewer white beans!) Pumpkin mac and cheese (why ruin the cheese?)—even if it was the powdery orange stuff Candice would never make at home, she made an exception at the food pantry since there was always a lot being donated. It wasn't like she was interested in any of my suggestions, so if you ask me, it was a huge waste of my time. Time

Candice and I could have been spending practicing with the bees.

I wasn't the only one getting stressed. Candice created a color-coded timeline of everything we needed to prepare before the festival. When we shared it with Mr. Henry and discussed how to get the bees to the festival, he had rubbed his chin a lot, but said transporting the bees wasn't going to be too bad. He'd feed them sugar syrup the night before so they'd be full and content. The biggest thing we had to worry about was the weather, and Mr. Henry said we'd need to be sure the bees didn't get agitated with the loud noises of the crowd.

Now that I had my own phone, Candice sent me about three texts an hour with reminders or random thoughts. I'd be seeing her in a few minutes at Mr. Henry's, but she sent me messages anyway.

Candice: We need a plan B. If it rains.

Like it did in 3rd grade.

Me: Okay! Trusty recorder to the rescue!

Candice: No offense, but NO!

Me: ????

Candice: We can still use the speech. Maybe add music to it?

Me: See! You do love my recorder!

OK, seriously. I'll finish the video to play behind us on

the curtain. It's easy. We used the website in coding club. Wanna help?

Candice: Yes! We'll start this afternoon after Mr. H.

I set my phone down at the front desk of the store and before I went to the website to choose a template for the video, I checked the store's e-mail. It was early and I'd come in to open the store with Dad while Fran went to a lifeguard training session at the crack of dawn.

Fifteen messages! Only three of the messages were spam. Twelve were orders for the desks. Two of those wanted the beds included. Dad had managed to get some good photos of the desks, some next to the beds, some alone.

It was working!

"Dad!" I called. The break room door was open a crack. Dad coughed a few times before coming out front.

"What's up, kiddo?"

His breath smelled too strongly of the mints he used to cover up his smoke breath. It was like when I could still taste raw onion through toothpaste when I ate too much salsa. Yuck.

Dad leaned over my shoulder. "Look at that." He slapped me on the back. "The golden ticket of sales is knowing what people need and giving them what they want."

Dad stared at me with a goofy grin. "Who knew the people needed desks!"

Fran pulled up outside the store and gave the horn a short, quick burst.

"You better get going," Dad said, settling into the chair as I got up. "I'll take care of these orders."

I slid into the backseat of Fran's car and barely had my seat belt on before she pulled back onto the road to get Candice. She was finally in a less monstrous mood, but she still treated Candice and me like *we* were the reason she was having a crappy week. I wanted to remind her that Mom was the one who'd gone away, leaving her in charge of getting us back and forth to Mr. Henry's since Dad had to be at the store by himself. It wasn't my idea.

I prepared to have to jump out quickly so Fran could speed away, but when we reached the top of Mr. Henry's driveway, he was sitting on the grass surrounded by pieces of wood. Some stuck straight up, the rest were still piled on the ground.

Fran shoved the car into park and didn't even bother turning it off. Candice and I jumped out after her and ran to him, half slipping in the still-dewy grass in the shade of the barn.

"Mr. Henry? Are you all right? Did you fall?" Fran asked, kneeling next to him.

"Good morning, ladies."

"Where's your wheelchair? Are you okay?" I asked.

Candice pointed to a walker. "You shouldn't be trying to walk without that, Mr. Henry."

"Oh, don't be so cautious. I had an appointment yesterday. The doctor said I needed to start using my legs or my ankle muscles wouldn't get strong again."

"Yes, but Mr. Henry, you should take it slowly. You could hurt it worse," Fran said.

It was nice to have Fran there, even if all that first-aid training from being a lifeguard had gotten to her head.

"I was just trying to bend down and get a few of these pieces of wood. Seems it's more of a two- or three-person job, in retrospect." He pushed himself up and Candice held the walker steady as he stood. "I was reviewing your research and the rules of the competition, and you have to have all your own props. I thought we'd better get started on building the bee beard cage."

Fran shook her head. "The what?"

"The bee beard cage. We need to get the wooden frame up by the end of the day. I'll buy a screen later so we can cover it."

"Yes, Mr. Henry. We'll be sure to get the hive all cleaned up," I said, hoping he'd stop talking about the bee bearding. Candice and I were so close to pulling off our talent, and I didn't want it to be ruined all because one of Fran's many talents of being a big sister included tattling.

Fran cocked her head at me in that big-sister you've-got-some-explaining-to-do angle. "Mr. Henry, why don't I stick around and help for today? I don't have to be at work."

"You just had training. Don't you need to go home and get a shower?" I asked, clenching my teeth. Usually after Fran swam laps all morning and "saved" the CPR dummies, she couldn't wait to shower and watch TV.

"No. I'm fine." She smiled, scrunching her nose and eyes.

"Well, your car is running. Still all nice and cool in there. Maybe you should just go home," I said.

"We could use the help," Mr. Henry said. "You girls get some clamps and extra hammers from the barn. I'll sketch out a plan."

Once we were at the car, Fran turned to Candice and me. "Bee beard? What are you guys up to?"

The car engine died, and Fran shoved the keys into her pocket.

"Oh. That?"

"Yes. *That*." Fran squinted at me, her eyes not once leaving mine.

I couldn't have Fran mess this up now. I had to make

her understand. "Fran, you said yourself that the recorder was a crappy talent."

"I never said 'crappy.'"

"It was all my idea," Candice butted in. "We need a talent that stands out if we want to win. We're not breaking any rules . . . exactly."

"Exactly?" Fran said. "You mean Mom and Dad have no idea, right?"

Neither Candice nor I answered.

"What if you get hurt?"

"We've been practicing," I said. "Mr. Henry's an expert. It's not even dangerous."

"It's true, Fran," Candice added. "Mr. Henry's had the bees for a long time and he knows what he's doing."

"Fran, please," I said. "Carissa's singing and guitar playing had everyone clapping. We can kick her butt."

"Well, I guess it would be nice to see Carissa lose."

"You're not going to tell Mom or Dad?"

Fran shook her head. "Not yet."

"Thanks, Fran." I lunged toward her and hugged her.

"You're doing my chores for two weeks."

"You're doing mine if you tell."

Fran rolled her eyes. "Deal."

Chapter Twenty-Two

Random Bee Fact #44:
Bees are attracted to carbon dioxide. Your breath is 4
percent carbon dioxide.

Fish Friday was the worst name Fran could have come up with for a day of the week most people looked forward to.

"I'll be back at eleven and you guys are going to help me pass out the tuna and cannellini bean fritter samples," Fran called through the window as she drove away, leaving Candice and me at the top of Mr. Henry's driveway.

Since Fran found out about our bee bearding talent she'd taken the opportunity to squeeze extra volunteer hours out of Candice and me. She dropped us off at Mr. Henry's every day to practice for an hour or two and then we'd spend the afternoons at the food pantry doing all the boring jobs like organizing cans or printing and cutting out recipes to put in holders by the shelves. In between all of this, I still had to dress up as a mattress and help Dad out at the store.

The hours we were at Mr. Henry's, we practiced the bee beard step by step, but still on my arm and with the netted hat. Mr. Henry wanted to be sure I was used to the feel of them and able to keep my muscles relaxed. I was getting used the soft but prickly way the bees clung to my arm.

We'd also helped Mr. Henry cover the wooden frame we built with a screen. He said most bee bearders used screened-in cages when large crowds were around to prevent unnecessary stings. This cage was a little taller than me and wide enough for me to have my hands on my hips and my elbows just touch the sides. A small stool fit inside so I could sit during the bee beard. A hinged door at the side allowed Mr. Henry to release the bees from the frame and close it so they stayed inside with me.

Practicing while squeezed inside the screened cage somehow made me feel smaller and the bees feel bigger, like one of those terrible sci-fi movies my dad would sometimes watch on a Saturday night, where insects towered over people. As a safety measure, Mr. Henry had also started to have us bring his leaf blower out from the barn when we practiced. It was a quick and harmless way to get the bees off, in case they started to sting.

"Well, let's get to it, girls," Mr. Henry called to Candice and me as he made his way down the ramp. He barely leaned on his walker, using it more like the way you'd push a vacuum in front of you. "This contest is only getting closer, and we've got to get this down to a science."

Candice and I grabbed everything we needed and met Mr. Henry at the hives. The bees had a smell I could recognize now. Like hot dirt, grass, and (maybe this was due to Fran's herbal invasion of our food) basil. More precisely lemon basil. How and why did I know the difference?

"We're going to practice today like you're at the festival. It's time to try the bee beard on your face, Florence." He pointed to the stool. "It'll be easier for you to stay still if you're sitting."

I knew this was coming and that I couldn't keep practicing with the bees on my arm, but a flutter ran through my body like my heart was beating at the speed of the bees' wings.

Mr. Henry separated the queen from a frame throbbing with wriggling bees as Candice smudged the thick, goopy Vaseline across my face, but not my chin.

Closeness was a weird thing. Yes, Candice was right in front of me, practically in my face, putting Vaseline carefully around my eyes and even on my eyebrows. She was so close I could see the three pimples that dotted across the dent below her bottom lip like a constellation. The Orion's Belt of pimples. But there was also the closeness of how we actually talked about things now. And, more surprisingly, how we *didn't* talk. Before, the silence between us fizzed like root beer in a root beer float—ready to overflow at any second. Lately, we'd kind of forgotten to keep busy and avoid each other. We could just be.

Once my face was sufficiently slimy I tore a few cotton balls into smaller pieces and put them in my ears and up my nose. Then, I used masking tape to stick my sleeves and collar to my skin, tucked my shirt into my leggings, and pulled socks over the bottoms. Anything to keep bees from getting into my clothes and then getting stuck. But my neck, arms, and face were bare and I was superaware of just how much skin was not covered. Especially now that I'd be trapped inside a screened-in cage with nowhere for me or the bees to escape.

I settled on a stool inside the cage as Mr. Henry handed the queen cage to Candice. Mr. Henry explained to her how to fasten the queen cage under my chin and let the string go over my ears so the queen would be up high for the beard.

The air was charged like just before a big summer

thunderstorm. I swear I could feel static build up as I waited for Mr. Henry to shake the bees from the frame. Mr. Henry stood next to the cage and held on to the doorframe as he angled the frame of bees toward me.

The minutes preparing for the bees made me swell with equal parts excitement and dread each time. This time felt bigger knowing they'd be on my face. Every single gurgle of my insides rang in my ears like I was suddenly a cave, echoing everything going on inside of me. As I waited for the bees to fumble toward me, looking for their queen, I felt like I needed to remind all my body parts that they really had to keep working.

Candice help up her phone. "I'll time it so I know how long to make my speech and see if we need to adjust the video."

"All right, here they come." Mr. Henry gave the tray a gentle fling in my direction.

The Vaseline blocked my sweat, making my skin feel fake and plastic.

The cotton balls up my nose made it feel like I couldn't catch my breath. I parted my lips slightly and sipped little bits of air in and leaked tiny bits out, afraid I'd suck a bee right into my mouth. When the bees were on my arm, I could see them, watch them, and I knew where they were. Waiting for them to land on my face filled me with the nervous excitement you get when playing hide-and-seek.

The bees didn't notice me at first. They bumbled around frantically, but the longer I watched them, the more I thought I understood them. They flew up and down and side to side, but somehow managed to make it look purposeful and graceful. There was a shift in their motion when they noticed where the queen was.

I could almost hear the change in their buzzing as they communicated to one another.

At least twenty bees swarmed my neck like a buzzing cloud. The bees' prickly legs landed for the tiniest fraction of a second before hopping off to find a part of my face without Vaseline.

The bees scrambled and hooked to one another, forming a clumsy, moving sheet against my face. Their buzzing and breathing fluttered against my skin, both soft and prickly.

"Excellent," Mr. Henry said under his breath. "I'll untie the queen cage. Once I take it off you can stand up and jump. Just like we practiced. Hard and fast."

The bees that pulsed under my chin clung to the queen cage as Mr. Henry untied it. The warmth of the other bees still tangled against my neck and in front of my ears like an itchy scarf.

"Okay," Mr. Henry said, opening the door and holding

the frame out like a platter just in front of me. I stood up and jumped, landing hard on my feet to knock the bees off. My teeth clattered together, but it worked. Most of the bees fell off of me, leaving me with a lightness like lifting the lead X-ray vest off my chest at the dentist.

Several bees straggled behind, still clinging to me. Waiting for them to notice that their friends were gone after being still for so long made the muscles in my neck and chest tighten. I couldn't wait to take a huge gulp of air.

Then, something sharp pricked the side of my chin.

My hands reacted more quickly than my brain. I smacked at the few bees still on my face even though I could hear Mr. Henry telling me to stay calm and stand still, but I just kept hopping up and down, whacking at the bees. My hand brushed against them, flinging them off of me. I didn't want to hurt them, but I didn't want them on my face, either. Another sting burned the palm of my hand.

Next thing I knew, a rush of air whipped my hair away from my face and puffed my cheeks out. The roar of the leaf blower startled me and I finally stood still, letting the rush of air get rid of the remaining bees.

Once the leaf blower had been turned off, I looked around and watched the bees that'd been blown off in the rush of air slowly make their way back to the hive.

I hated that I'd slapped at the bees. I knew not to. It wasn't the bees' fault.

"Well, that was eventful," Mr. Henry said.

I yanked my leggings out of my socks and untucked my shirt. I would have yanked the hairband out from my ponytail, too, if it wasn't so humid that my hair would react like a static-electricity experiment gone wrong.

"Hey, don't worry. Better it happened now so if it happens again you'll be prepared," Candice said.

I nodded, rubbing at the pulsing sting on my chin. It was one of those things like getting a shot. You tell yourself it doesn't hurt, but you still tense up and flinch when it happens. As long as I didn't flinch onstage, no one would know if I'd been stung.

I had a crown to win, and for the first time a surge of hope rushed through me, telling me I might have a chance to actually pull it off.

Chapter Twenty-Three

Random Bee Fact #62:
A Challenger flight took 3,300 bees to space. The bees adapted to zero gravity and built a nearly normal hive, but didn't use the bathroom for the entire month they were in space.

A larger than normal group got off the train Saturday.

Antiquers.

I flipped the sign from CLOSED to OPEN.

"Flor, suit up. Make sure they see us. They might need a new mattress for the new old bed they buy." He nudged me and laughed at his own joke.

It was already muggy with the break room door propped open into the parking lot to get rid of the burned-popcorn smell that still filled the store after Dad overmicrowaved a bag of popcorn for his lunch the day before. Dad wasn't much of a cook, even when the food came with simple heating instructions.

I stepped into the mattress suit already sweaty but wanting to help Dad any way I could.

The bells over the door jangled, and Mrs. Thorton's voice started before they had a chance to stop.

"Did you receive this notice too?" she asked, pushing a paper across the counter. The words *Thorton's Landscaping: Leaf it to Us!* on her T-shirt stretched and contracted with each breath. "Rents are going up twenty percent. That's double the usual."

Dad cleared his throat. I couldn't make out his answer.

"How will you manage?" she asked. "Your father started this store thirty years ago. I can't imagine it not being here."

I wanted to step out of the break room and hear what Dad was saying, but Mrs. Thorton might stop talking if I did, and I wanted to hear whatever I could. Helping was becoming more complicated, not to mention more expensive. What if winning wasn't enough? How many desks would we have to sell?

"That Clarence Henry sure is a tyrant when he wants to be," Mrs. Thorton said, her hand smacking down on the front counter.

I sucked in a breath so quickly I had to swallow down a cough. Clarence? Henry? Mr. Henry? Stupid mattress costume eyeholes. I leaned my body against the door and angled my head just so, and I could see through the crack in the door.

"I didn't mean to meddle, but your mom and dad were such a big part of this town. I asked Florence to help Clarence out. I thought for sure once he met your Florence he'd soften and back off. Realize what a nice family you all are."

I thought back to that day Mrs. Thorton had come in here and I signed those papers. She and Mom gave each other a look when Mrs. Thorton said Mr. Henry's name.

I could only see the back of Dad's shoulder as he said, "I sent in a complaint, but the Historical Society is pressuring him to make upgrades that aren't cheap." The heaviness of his voice made me feel tired.

I turned so I could lean my back against the wall next to the door, but being a walking mattress, I couldn't quite tell where I was leaning and leaned against the door instead, falling right out of the break room and onto the floor behind where Dad was standing at the counter.

Mrs. Thorton jumped back. "Gracious!"

"Flor? You okay?" Dad reached down to help me up.

"Fine!" I yelled, the words bouncing right back in my face. I wasn't fine.

"See you both at the ball next week," Mrs. Thorton said in the same overly chipper tone I'd used to say I was fine. She leaned in closer to Dad and said, "Let me know if I can help." The bells clanged as the store door closed behind her.

"Mr. Henry?" I asked Dad, unable to get any more words out of my mouth.

Dad rubbed the back of his neck and shrugged. "He owns more than half the buildings in town."

"Our store, too?"

Dad nodded. "Yes, our store, too."

I shook my head. Before I knew him as Mr. Henry, I knew him only as the Old Man on the Hill, not sure if he really existed. Then I met him covered in bees. And he'd ordered Candice and me around until he wasn't a scary old man, but just Mr. Henry. The guy who helped us build a bee beard cage and patiently taught me how to let them on my face.

"I'll talk to him, Dad. I've been up there every week for over a month and—"

"I have already talked to him, Florence."

"But, if he knows . . ." The rest of the sentence stuck somewhere between my chest and my throat.

Mr. Henry knew who I was. He knew Gramps. He knew Dad was running the store. He knew things weren't going well.

184

He didn't care.

"You can't let him get away with this." I squeezed my hands into fists. They were about the only part of my body I could move exactly how I wanted to when I was trapped inside the mattress. "You can't just let this happen and not do anything. You always say we'll live to sell another day."

Still upset, I shoved out the door. I could try to sell mattresses even if Dad was just going to give up. I paced up and down the sidewalk in front of the store, chasing any sliver of shade I could find. Not that the shade would cool me down. I was covered in the kind of sweat that came from somewhere deep inside me, not from the heat.

The only good thing about being trapped in a mattress suit was that I could let the thoughts that were coiled like a skein of yarn unwind inside my head all in the privacy of a stuffed costume.

Dad was just going to let Mr. Henry raise rents without putting up a fight. The next time I saw Mr. Henry, I was going to tell him just what I thought. Dad said he'd talked to him, but he must not have been clear enough. I'd been around Mr. Henry all summer. Candice and I'd convinced him of the bee-bearding plan, so I knew I could get him to back down on the rent. At least until we sold enough desks to make up for the slowness of the past few months.

I felt a punch in the middle of my back. I turned

around. It was a little kid, probably six or seven. The rest of his family were staring in the windows of the museum and not at all watching their bratty kid.

He pulled his leg back to kick me.

"Don't even think about it," I said.

"Pillows can't talk," he said. But it came out more like "Piwwos can't tock."

"*Mattress*. I'm a mattress." Annoyance burned through each word. I pointed toward his family. "Uh-oh, your mom's coming."

He turned to look and see if I was telling the truth, and just at that moment, Mr. Henry stepped out of the jewelry store, leaning on a cane. Of course he had money to buy gold after practically stealing from my family. All those rumors about him murdering Girl Scouts and pizza delivery guys might not be true, but he was forcing my family to give up and run off to New Jersey.

Before the bratty kid could figure out I'd lied about his mom coming and actually kick me, I walked toward the traffic light and punched the crosswalk button.

I marched across the street, my feet hitting the ground faster than the green man could blink. I might have heard Dad yell after me, but I only had one thing on my mind, and that was to give a piece of it to Mr. Henry.

Mr. Henry leaned against his cane in front of the

Chocolate Factory. The sweet, deep smells of the hand-dipped chocolate, caramel, and pecan turtles were no distraction to me. Okay, maybe a little bit. You couldn't stand in front of that store and not be distracted. I swallowed down the rich smells and stopped right in front of Mr. Henry.

"It's *your* fault." The words spluttered out of my mouth like accidental spit.

"Excuse me?" Mr. Henry's mouth opened and closed.

"It's you, Mr. Henry. You're the reason my dad's store is doing so badly my mom wants us to move to New Jersey."

"Florence?" Mr. Henry squinted and ducked to see if he could glimpse me inside the stupid mattress.

I closed my eyes because seeing his face scrunched like he was confused made my voice come out quieter, reminding me of the past few weeks as he helped Candice and me. "You can't raise our rent."

"Young lady, things are more complicated than you know. The plumbing and electricity of those buildings are so old and it costs a pretty penny to keep that brick from crumbling."

Crumbling. The only thing crumbling was my life. The words clogged my throat and I couldn't even swallow them down or push them out angry and hot like they burned sitting in my chest.

"You can't do this," I said. "Why? Why did you . . ." I felt the fight drain out of me. My voice kind of gave up and came out as a whisper. "After everything this summer. You knew my dad's store was having trouble. And now, thanks to you, it doesn't matter what I do. Nothing will save it now."

"Business is business, Florence. If I let your father get away with not paying rent, I'd have to let everyone get away with it."

"Well, *you're* not going to get away with it. You'll be sorry." I turned to walk away, but stopped. It was like whenever I got into a fight with Fran and knew I was wrong, but still added one more jab just to feel like I was right. But I actually felt right this time. He might not have known I wanted to use the prize money to help the store, but he did know who my dad was. "Don't expect me to come all the way up that hill anymore."

I stomped away, feeling like a five-year-old. What did Mr. Henry care if I stopped coming to his house? It was difficult enough to see through the poorly placed eyeholes of the mattress costume, and with tears stinging my eyes, making my vision so blurry all I could see were blobs of color as I walked away from Mr. Henry and back toward the store.

"Florence," Dad's voice was light, but firm and comforting like one of his mattresses. I lunged toward him to hug him, but forgot I was still in the costume and fell onto the sidewalk on my side.

"Well, that's not good for business," Dad said, laughing.

It wasn't even funny, but laughing at his lame joke beat crying over mean Mr. Henry.

Dad helped me up and I leaned against him as we walked back across the street. "Maybe your mom's right," he said, stopping in front of the store.

I could just make out Dad's chin. "Right about what?"

"Hanging on to this store. Staying in this town. Your mom's a smart lady," he said.

"She doesn't know everything," I said.

"Flor, she's been trying to call you all day. Have you checked your phone?"

I shrugged the question off.

"She wanted to tell you herself that she got the job."

Anger filled me fast and burning-hot. Dad stood there, his face not exactly sad or happy. It rested somewhere in between.

I didn't want to leave Honeydale, but I was the only one fighting to stay. What if—no! I cut off any thought that giving up was an option.

The festival wasn't over yet.

Chapter Twenty-Four

Random Bee Fact #49:
Honey is basically nectar vomited out of a bee's special
nectar-only stomach. It gets thick and sticky as the water
evaporates from the heat of the hive.

I rummaged through the cupboards until I found a lunch-box-size applesauce behind a box of a Fran-approved version of my favorite sugary cereal. The applesauce was lukewarm, making it taste sour.

It was fitting. Mom had called me again last night, but I'd let it add to the number of missed calls next to her name. I already knew what she was going to say, so why did I have to answer just to hear her be excited that she was ruining my life?

I shoveled in the last few bites of applesauce and opened

up my messages. It was time to write Brooke. I broke the past two months up in little chat-size pieces: Candice and me helping Fran and discovering bee beards. Mom off in New Jersey probably finding a house now that the job was for sure. Mr. Henry as landlord, raising rents.

It felt good to let her know everything. Finally.

I held my phone, hoping Brooke would message me back, but gave up after a few minutes. Moving to New Jersey suddenly felt like a Thing. A Thing that would really happen, no longer just a possibility.

I didn't know if that made things easier or harder.

The library was quiet. It was the earliest I'd ever been there. I'd even waited outside for about ten minutes before they unlocked the doors. Mrs. Thorton had asked all the contestants to arrive at nine thirty, but I needed to get away from Dad even if it meant wandering the library by myself for thirty minutes. I'd told him I had to help set up for craft hour, which I did, just not this early.

I walked up and down the aisles, running my hand along the neatly lined books. The stillness felt like a deep breath of fresh air. At the end of an aisle filled with thick art books hung a large portrait of a woman with long brown hair, smiling with her head tilted slightly to the side. A gold plaque at the bottom of the frame read:

Marjorie Henry (1946–2005)
The Marjorie Henry Wing of the Library
Dedicated by Clarence Henry

The skin on my arms tingled. The same nervousness I got when surrounded by bees filled me right then.

Mr. Henry's wife.

Being able to put a face to a person I'd never met, and never would, made her real in a way that sent sadness through me like I'd actually known her.

I just couldn't figure out who Mr. Henry was. The pieces of him didn't fit neatly together. The calm Mr. Henry bee-man and the greedy landlord Mr. Henry didn't completely mix into something that made sense.

The click of folding tables opening came from near the children's section of the library. Time to set up for craft hour.

Only Mrs. Thorton and Carissa were there. Seeing Carissa reminded me that Candice and my chance of winning now were pretty much over. And plus I kept picturing her with Josh near the CPR dummies. Eww.

"Morning, Mrs. Thorton," I said as I walked into the children's section.

"You're early," Carissa said, her face stiff, not giving away a single bit of the annoyance obvious from her voice.

Mrs. Thorton shoved a pile of papers into my arms. "Here. Help me organize the tables."

Our craft was an educational project about bees for kids. The top paper was in the shape of a cartoon beehive. The bottom paper was a circle the kids could cut out and attach behind the hive with a brad to spin and explain each life stage of the bee. Candice arrived a few minutes later along with a few of the other contestants, but Mrs. Thorton had us all so busy taping on tablecloths and finding containers for the safety scissors that we couldn't stop until ten minutes before craft hour was to begin.

We were all going to sit with the kids through story time and then do the craft when the story was over. We helped Mrs. Madison set out the beanbags and carpet squares and soon the little kids arrived with their parents. Some of the parents sat down with their kids; others hung around the edges.

Mrs. Thorton shooed us to go sit among the kids and talk. Candice looked terrified. "They're just little kids," I whispered.

"I'm afraid they'll start crying."

Candice was weird about little kids? I never knew that.

Candice clung close to me. I tried to talk to the little girl next to me, but she just shook or nodded her head. Finally the librarian began to read a story about a bee living on a farm and then it was time for the craft.

Carissa took the lead and showed the kids what the

completed craft looked like. The kids spread out over the two tables and we handed them the supplies they needed. The kids worked pretty quietly and didn't really need much help.

"Candice," I whispered. "We need to talk after this."

"About what?" she asked, popping the cap off a pink marker for the shy girl from story time. She insisted her beehive be pink.

"Just festival stuff."

"Oh, I was thinking we could video your bee beard. That way if it rains or something happens we can mix it in with the movie."

"About that." I pushed a brad through the craft for a little boy and handed it back to him. "I'm not sure we can use the bees anymore."

Candice whipped her head toward me; the scissors in the jar rattled against one another. "What are you talking about?" Candice leaned in closer.

"Mr. Henry owns a bunch of buildings, and he's raising the rents. He's the reason my dad's store is losing money."

"Okay." Candice let the words stretch over a few seconds like she was waiting for me to explain more.

"Candice, don't you get it? I asked him to not raise rents and he had some excuse about pipes and bricks falling. So I told him I never want to see him again."

I waited for what I'd said to click and for Candice to let me know I'd done the right thing and Mr. Henry was horrible.

The little boy in front of me reached his hand up for the scissors, waiting for Candice to pass him a pair. Candice was still staring at me, so I reached for a pair and passed it to him.

"You told him *what?*" Candice barely whispered.

"He can't raise rents."

"No, the other thing."

"I never want to see him ever again."

"Florence." Candice shook her head.

I didn't miss that she called me "Florence," like we'd gone from friends back to enemies in a single moment.

"Rents aren't what's ruining your dad's store. You said sales have been down since before the summer."

"Yeah, but paying more money every month isn't going to help."

Candice pointed right at my chest. "You do realize he's the key to our talent, right? Do you even get that this isn't just about you?" Her voice was definitely not "library polite" like the poster behind her stated.

I glanced over at where Carissa and Mrs. Thorton were standing. Mrs. Thorton and the librarian were chatting, but Carissa watched us closely.

"What's that supposed to mean?" My voice scratched my throat as I tried to keep it a whisper.

"You just ruined our chances of winning. Not just yours, but *ours*. You're impossible."

"I was only trying to—"

Candice put up her hand. "Look, I'm sorry about your dad's store, but it's not Mr. Henry's fault. It *is* your fault that we're both going to lose now. After all the research, time practicing, and even making that movie."

"But we can still do the speech and the movie or our duet."

Candice shoved the jar into my hands and rushed out the library doors.

Boiling-hot tears squeezed out the sides of my eyes. I wiped them away faster than they could fall.

Candice didn't think any of this was Mr. Henry's fault. Even Dad didn't blame him.

So I stood there, clutching a jar of safety scissors, feeling as dry and crumbly as one of Fran's granola bars.

Chapter Twenty-Five

Random Bee Fact #7:
Bees that are not protecting their hives or their honey
store aren't a threat and usually don't sting.

Expecting Fran to side with me was always a stretch, but she didn't even act surprised when I told her how Candice had stormed out of craft hour.

When she finally did turn around, all she said was, "Can you do something useful? You're just sitting there." Fran spread her arms out. "Start sorting the piles of mail and clean up. Mom and Dad'll be back from the airport soon."

I grabbed one of the stacks of mail scattered on the counter and put them in a single pile next to the fridge. "What else was I supposed to do?"

"Flor, I'm sorry, but Candice is right. You're selfish."

It wasn't like it was a surprise that both my frenemy and my sister thought I was selfish. I started piles for bills and junk and personal mail. "How is telling Mr. Henry I don't want to see him selfish?"

"Because Candice is actually serious about winning and you took away her chance."

I wanted to disagree with her, but I might have been the one who was letting the bees crawl all over me, but Candice was the one who knew so much about them. She was the one who wanted to be a bee ambassador. All I wanted was the cash. Now, the cash didn't mean anything. "Oh," I said, grabbing a handful of cashews. "So I'll just drop out. She can play piano. Use the projection movie."

"Seriously? What don't you get about selfish?" Fran asked.

"I said she can use the projection movie. That took me, like, three hours."

"Flor, you can't just drop her. You have to do this with her."

"What's the point? We don't have the bees. We can't win."

"It doesn't matter if *you* win." Fran stared at me the way she watched her rice-paper fake bacon in the oven so it didn't burn. She was studying me. Waiting for something to happen.

Oh. Right. "Candice could still win this."

Fran nodded. "Duh. Now stop eating all the cashews. I need them for the sauce."

If Candice was going to win, I had to get those bees back.

I leaned against the counter. Mom and Dad were coming back from the airport any minute. Somehow knowing Mom was going to walk through the door made moving feel more real. More than getting news that she'd gotten the job. "So, it's final now?" I asked Fran.

"I guess so."

"You're okay with it?" I asked, frustrated that I felt betrayed. Not just by Mom and Mr. Henry, but by my feelings. Like I should also be okay with moving if I was more mature like Fran.

Fran scraped a pile of sliced mushrooms into a bowl and set down the knife and cutting board. She leaned onto the counter and touched the top of her head to mine. "I don't know. Maybe it'll be good. I looked up the school and it looks cool. They offer college credit courses and I can even create my own personal independent study class and keep developing my affordable healthy-eating program."

"Surprise!" Dad called as the back door opened.

I pushed myself up out of the chair and walked slowly toward the door.

Mom and Gram walked into the kitchen both holding out their arms.

"Gram! Mom!" I ran to them both, letting their arms pull me in.

"Get over here, Fran," Gram called.

"Gram wanted to surprise you girls," Dad said. "Her flight from Florida arrived an hour before mom's."

All through dinner Mom was happier than I'd seen her in a long time. I'd forgotten how bright her eyes got when she smiled with more than just her mouth.

It was nice to have Gram there to fill in the all the quiet gaps with talk of Florida and not about the store or Mom's new job, even though it was all I was thinking about.

After we'd washed the dinner dishes, Gram held up her knitting and asked me to bring a crochet project and meet her out on the back porch.

We sat side by side on the porch swing Gramps had built when I was five. The rhythmic *screech-scrooch* of the chains as we rocked and the clicking of Gram's knitting needles made it feel right to sit quietly. So we did. I looped and hooked, trying out a new wristband pattern that looked like several small bracelets attached together at the clasp.

After several minutes, Gram put her knitting in her lap and took a long drink of iced tea. "Your grandfather started that store on a whim." She rested the cup between us, making a ring of water form on the wood of the swing. "He was always getting one idea after another. Finally, I'd had enough. I told him that was the last idea and he had to stick with it." She shook her head, making the swing rock diagonally. "It's not the store that matters, Flor. Closing the store won't make any difference to your Gramps now. But you know what would?"

She waited for me to look over at her. When I did, she patted my cheek. "Your happiness and well-being."

We rocked for a minute longer before she added, "Your mom and dad want the best for you and Fran. If I can move and make new friends as an old lady, Flor, you can do it better and faster than I can."

I nodded, but tears threatened to spill out. Not the hot, angry kind I'd been fighting back all summer, but sad, finished tears. Finished like maybe moving and a new house and a new school in New Jersey wouldn't be so bad. It was the new friends I wasn't so sure about.

I was sitting on my bed, torturing myself by staring at my phone, waiting for a message from Brooke to pop up. I messaged her again about Gram being here and asked what time she was getting back the next day.

My door opened a crack. "Florence?" Mom didn't say

it in the tone she usually saved for using my full name. She said it soft and whispery.

My stomach turned in the way it did when Fran left chopped-up fruit and vegetable scraps in a tin next to the sink. Not because Mom smelled like slowly rotting beetroot and spring onions, but because I felt like compost for avoiding her phone calls while she'd been gone.

I shoved my phone under my pillow and said, "Come in."

"You and Gram have a good talk?" Mom asked, grabbing my feet and putting them on her lap as she sat on my bed. She cleared her throat and stared at the carpet in my room for a minute before saying, "I'm sorry. I know you want to stay."

I twisted my fingers together and waited for the "but." "But you'll understand when you're older" or "But it's what's best."

Mom didn't say any of that. Instead she said, "You must have been busy. You never answered my calls."

I picked at my wristband. "Candice and I had a lot to do." I wanted to avoid this conversation, especially after talking with Gram. The surprise of her arrival and the talk with her left my eyes feeling like a wet sponge, heavy and ready to drip. I wanted to wait until after I was in bed to cry.

Mom tickled the tops of my feet the way she did when we watched TV. "I just wanted to let you know that we didn't make this decision lightly." Mom stopped talking and turned to look at me. "I'm going to miss Honeydale. I'm even going to miss the store despite the headache it's given us. But, Flor, this isn't the end of Honeydale, Ohio, for us. Just consider this move a new chapter."

I nodded along, because what else was I supposed to do?

"Well, I hope you're not busy tomorrow. We should really go dress shopping for your festival dress. I thought we could shop downtown and get lunch at Aunt Bee's."

"I promised Dad I'd help out in the mattress costume."

"We'll go after mattress duty," Mom said. "Oh, and I invited Brooke and her family around for a barbeque this weekend. Have you said anything to her yet?"

I nodded my head slowly. A rush of tears felt like they started in my chest and were racing for my eyes, but I pushed them back. She still hadn't replied.

"You and Brooke have something special. Moving will change things, but it won't end things. You have your phone now and you've survived the summer apart."

I nodded again, but I wasn't really sure why. Brooke would be back in hours, no longer weeks or days, and she hadn't messaged or called. I didn't buy into that whole distance-makes-the-heart-grow-fonder crap. Brooke had been away all summer and I'd never felt farther away from her than now. Where was she?

Chapter Twenty-Six

Random Bee Fact #55:
When trained, bees are able to recognize and remember
one human face from another.

An hour before Brooke's family arrived, I slipped onto the hammock Dad finally strung up. I leaned back and swung myself with my foot that I kept hanging off the side. Brooke had called last night. She'd lost her charger and now she didn't have her phone until she earned enough money by filing at her dad's office to pay for a new charger.

Brooke hadn't seen any of my messages. I had to tell her about moving to her face. After weeks of being unsure how to text her the news, I was definitely not prepared to say it out loud.

What if she wasn't as sad as me when I told her about moving? What if this summer was exactly what I'd feared: an apple to the head? It had just been that kind of summer and . . . what if things weren't done getting worse?

Gram made the baked beans how I liked them—with extra brown sugar. I'd helped her ice her famous chocolate cake. She'd promised to save me an extra-large slice for later if I needed it.

I let the smoky smells of the grill waft over me as I rocked back and forth, lost in a cloud of thoughts. It wasn't long before I heard Brooke's younger brothers talking in their too-loud voices and car doors closing. Brooke's brothers Sam and Ben reached me first, holding up bug houses for later, when the lightning bugs came out.

Brooke hung back, waiting for them to finish showing me how to open and close the boxes before their mom called them over to her. Then there was nothing and an entire summer of everything between Brooke and me.

Brooke moved first and next thing I knew I was silent-crying into her shoulder. "Why is everyone acting so weird?" Brooke asked into my hair. "Mom was telling Ben and Sam to give us time, and she never does that." Brooke pulled out of the hug. "And now you're crying. What's going on?"

I shook my head and wiped the tears away with the back of my hand.

"Wait a minute. Am I going to need brownies for this? Please say yes. My mom made an entire platter and I'm so sick of camp food."

"I missed you," I said, laughing. Only Brooke could turn the worst thing ever into something funny.

We sneaked a napkin full of brownies off the platter her mom had put on the table near the grill and scrambled up the crab apple tree that hung over my driveway before her brothers could find us.

"So, spill," Brooke said, shoving a brownie in her mouth.

"My mom got a job in New Jersey and we're moving in two weeks before school starts. I thought I could stop it from happening, but that didn't work out." I told Brooke about Mr. Henry, the bees, Candice, even about Mom and Dad.

Brooke held up her hands. "Wait a minute. This happened in the last two *months* or have I been gone for years?"

It had felt like this summer was somehow in slow-motion and superspeed at the same time.

"Why didn't you call me? I could have helped you." Brooke shoved a bite of one of her three brownies in her mouth. "You know, Mr. Henry comes into my dad's. He told me Mr. Henry is super-rich. He invented a machine to make the tops of pop cans and then he researched diseases."

"Mr. Henry gets his teeth cleaned at your dad's?"

"Yeah, sure," Brooke said through another mouthful of brownie.

"What kind of stuff did he research?"

"I don't know. Something with goats and bees. Don't ask me how my dad can understand people when he's got all those instruments in their mouths," Brooke said, still chewing her brownie.

"I think I have a good idea how," I said, talking like I had my mouth full of brownie, too.

Brooke stuck out her tongue before shoving another big bite of brownie in her mouth, making me laugh. She leaned closer, resting her head on my shoulder. When she chewed the brownie, her jaw moved my arm just a little.

The sun hung low in the sky and the clouds from earlier seemed to have trapped all the heat, making my skin sticky. Brooke's hair tickled the side of my face, but I couldn't bring myself to move. If I did, she'd lift her head and this moment would be over.

"New Jersey. That's close enough to New York," Brooke said. "You know, when I get all famous and I'm living in the big city, I'll come visit you."

"I'll help you file at your dad's office so you can get your phone back faster."

"I was so annoyed. I plugged it in the main hall one night during talent hour and I forgot about it. No one ever turned it in to the Lost and Found."

She continued to tell me about camp. The way our conversation had slipped into such a normal back-and-forth, moving didn't feel real.

"Girls, dinner," Dad called.

Everyone else was already seated at the table outside. Brooke and I squished next to each other at the end, our elbows knocking into each other as we reached for scoops of potato salad and tomato slices and lettuce for our burgers.

Ben and Sam's silly jokes filled up all the unsaid worries and what-ifs between Brooke and me.

We caught lightning bugs with Ben and Sam and eventually lay sideways on the hammock thinking about good-bye, but not once saying it.

Later, in bed, I grabbed my phone and Googled Mr. Henry. I couldn't get the inventor-slash-researcher stuff Brooke had said out of my head. There were a few articles listed. One even in the *New York Times* a few years ago.

Clarence Henry (1944–present) lives in Honeydale, Ohio, where he once ran the Henry Corporation,

*which produced pop tabs for canned drinks on a
machine he invented himself. Henry has several
other patents on farm and agricultural equipment
as well as for livestock antibiotics. He recently
sold his company to Kline Manufacturers in
order to pursue full-time research on multiple
sclerosis (MS) with the use of bees and goat's milk
products. Henry's research using goat's milk as
a possible supplement for symptom reversal for
patients suffering from MS had started to gain
credibility just before his late wife, Marjorie, died
after suffering complications from relapsing-
remitting MS (RRMS), the most common form
of MS. Henry hopes to find a cure for the disease
through the use of bee venom. The research is not
new, but Henry hopes that through funding he
can expand the study.*

All I could picture was Mr. Henry all alone up on that
hill. When Gramps died, Gram moved in with us for a few
months. She couldn't stand to be alone in her house with
Gramps not there. Then she sold the house and moved to
Florida. She surrounded herself with people. Mr. Henry
hid himself away.

Another piece of the Mr. Henry puzzle.

I wondered if Candice knew bee venom could possibly cure multiple sclerosis. She needed to add this to her speech—if I could convince her to still do it. And if I could convince Mr. Henry to forgive me.

Chapter Twenty-Seven

Random Bee Fact #3:
A bee colony can only have one queen at a time. If another queen is born, they fight to the death.

Candice refused to answer my calls, even when I sent her a text saying it was urgent. It was the day of our last event before the festival, the annual fund-raising ball for multiple sclerosis. Mr. Henry had to be going. It would be my chance to say sorry and get the bees back.

The ball wasn't until after dinner, so Mom gave me a list of chores to do beforehand. She'd had boxes delivered and Gram was helping her pack the kitchen while Fran cleaned out closets. In Cinderella fashion, I dusted and vacuumed the entire house before it was time to get ready.

Fran offered to let me borrow one of her old home-coming dresses for the ball, but "ball" wasn't the kind of word you heard every day unless you were reading a fairy tale. Fran's homecoming dresses were okay, but didn't feel very "dream come true." And right then, I wanted to feel like anything was possible.

The only dressy thing I had was the lehenga I wore two summers ago for a wedding. The skirt had dragged against the ground even when Mom pulled it up and tied it around my ribs under its top to make it shorter. It only took a few minutes for the weight of the beading to pull it back down. I had to lift it to walk. It fit perfectly now, but I decided to wear one of Fran's sequined tank tops with it because the lehenga tops are kind of like crop tops, and even though the skirt fit, the top was way too cropped now.

The lehenga skirt was navy and embroidered from the waist to the thick border at the bottom with sparkly copper swirls and sequins. The border had a copper trim and dark pink embroidered flowers with so many beads I had to kick it as I walked. The dark pink sparkles on Fran's tank top matched it perfectly.

The easy part was getting dressed. The hard part was getting my hair and the rest of me to be as fancy as what I was wearing.

I went outside her room and hovered near the door,

wanting Fran to notice me so I wouldn't have to actually ask for help.

"Oh, Flor, you're hopeless," Fran said when she looked up from the pile of clothes she was sorting into boxes. "Only you could take the cutest outfit and make it look sloppy." She grabbed my arms and pulled me back to my room. "Look. Half of wearing something nice is standing like you're wearing it, not like it weighs a million pounds." She held me by the shoulders in front of the full-length mirror on my closet door. "Straighten your back." Fran pushed against my spine. "You can*not* use this chalky deodorant. You already got smudges over here. I'll get my clear glide. But, before we even get to the deodorant, we've got to do something with your hair." Fran shoved me onto the bench seat in front of my desk.

I tried to sit still as she held my hair in different positions. Up. Down. On the side. On the other side. Half up. Half down. All up.

It was easier to sit still with bees crawling on my face than it was to let Fran tangle up my hair.

"Okay. I suggest we pull your hair over to the side like this, but leave this part down."

Fran stared in the mirror with her head to one side, waiting for my opinion. I expected to hate it and not feel like myself, but it actually looked all right. I was surprised, because I didn't think I could pull off a fancy hairstyle. It didn't look or feel half as fussy as I imagined.

I kept my mouth shut as Fran held my hair in place and dug around for bobby pins in the accessory bag she'd brought from her room. Even when the bobby pins poked my scalp and scraped my skin, I just made my grimace into a smile because I actually believed that she wasn't doing this on purpose.

I tipped my head side to side and patted at my hair, just to make sure it was secure enough to stay in place.

"Don't touch," Fran said, smacking my hand away.

I blinked and squinted as she dabbed some pink tint on my lips and cheeks and brushed my lashes with mascara, brightening my face.

"How'd you learn to do this?" I asked, surprised that I no longer felt or looked like a little kid dressed like an adult.

"It's a gift," Fran said with an exaggerated flutter of her eyelashes. "But really, you just have to know what colors work with your skin." She grabbed a smaller brush and held it in front of me. "This is for the creases in your eyes. This part here." She brushed it against my eyelid at the top of my eyeball. "Use a darker shade here, then choose a lighter shade for the rest of your lid." Fran brushed more sparkly copper on my lids and touched up my mascara.

"You have the best lashes. You could do this every day, just without the lipstick. Save that for special occasions," Fran said, standing back and looking at my reflection.

"Thanks," I said. I really meant it, but the temperature change with Fran could shift as quickly as a cold snap in the spring that leaves behind frost so I added, "You know, for sharing your gift."

Fran studied my reflection in the mirror for a minute, like she saw more than a brighter face and smoother hair. Her eyes went deeper than that, like she thought of me differently, no longer just as a little sister. "I have something for you," she said. "Just a minute." She ran off to her room and came back with the sparkly silver clutch she'd taken to prom a few months ago.

"What is it?"

"Okay, well, I was going to save it for the festival, but why wait. Just open it."

I took the bag from her and unzipped it. There were tiny bottles and some tinted lip gloss. Kylie Jenner brand. I set the bag on my lap and looked up at Fran, still holding the lip gloss. "This must have been at least an entire day of sunbathing to buy this," I said, trying to make a joke.

"Ha-ha. It's called life-saving, not sunbathing," she said.

I pulled out all the bottles, inspecting each one.

Fran snatched the bottles from me, opening them one

by one and telling me what was inside. "Vaseline. Cotton balls. This one is an apple cider vinegar and lavender oil thing I made. If you put it on some cotton balls it'll take the Vaseline right off. The other ones you can shove up your nose or whatever it is you do. And last"—she paused to pull out a pair of earrings—"the turquoise earrings Great-Gram gave me. They'll look very boho with your dress. And it all fits in here perfectly."

She handed the clutch back to me, saying, "You're welcome," before I could form a proper thank-you.

"But I haven't even asked Mr. Henry yet about the bees."

"For someone brave enough to let a bunch of bees on your face, you sure are a baby about asking a question."

Chapter Twenty-Eight

Random Bee Fact #89:
Bees can't see red—it looks like black to them—so they
don't pollinate red flowers.

I was used to seeing Dad in shorts with the most frus-
trating white socks that had a thick red or navy stripe
across the top. At least he wore pants to work that hid
the socks. But seeing him in a suit and tie was like looking
at a photo from a magazine with his head pasted on. The
only time I'd seen him in a suit outside of a picture was at
Gramps's funeral. But I'd been too upset that day to appreciate how good he looked.

Dad turned on the classical music station as we drove
downtown to the Golden Lamb, the brick building across
the street from the library. It'd been around since Abraham

Lincoln was president. He even visited there during his campaign way back a long time ago. It used to be one of the fanciest hotels and restaurants around, but now it was just a restaurant.

The function room downstairs smelled like a musty basement. Even disguised with twinkling lights, the floors creaked enough and slanted in the corners that you knew you were in a superold building. After a few minutes I got used to the smell and could actually appreciate the decorations. Tiny fresh white flowers filled vases on every table. The same flowers were strung across the ceiling, intertwined with the lights.

Dad nudged me. "This old place never looked so good."

I nodded and followed him to our table. The tables were arranged at the edges of the room and the center was left empty for dancing. I could dance in a fun, goofoff way, but I really hoped they wouldn't have us do a father-daughter thing to slow music. I scanned the room for Candice or Mr. Henry, but didn't see either of them anywhere.

I grabbed some punch for Dad and stood around awkwardly beside him as he and a few of the other dads chatted about sports and work until Mrs. Thorton waved the contestants over. Candice hovered near Mrs. Thorton, avoiding looking at me. It wasn't even one of those kinds of avoiding where you look when the other person isn't looking and look away quickly when they do. Candice was full-on staring at Mrs. Thorton and pretending each word she said was the most important thing in the world, when really all she was telling us was to walk around the room, selling raffle tickets and Honey Festival pens and small jars of local honey for donations.

I grabbed my basket and hurried after Candice. She was stopped by a couple wanting to buy some pens and a raffle ticket. I hung back, impatient for them to let her go so I could talk to her about Mr. Henry.

The room filled up with more people I didn't know than people I did.

Just as Candice finished up with the couple, I got stopped and had to sell a few. I managed to keep Candice just in my sights until the music started. It was just a small band with a piano, drums, and guitar, but the room shrunk in around me and I had to be sure to lift my lehenga skirt with one hand as I moved around. Next thing I knew, Candice was nowhere in sight. I lifted up on my toes to try to find her light brown hair, but the twinkling lights made everyone's hair look colorless.

I crashed back onto my feet with a sigh and turned around, bumping right into someone.

"Sorry," I said, leaning down to pick up the raffle tickets that had fallen out of my basket.

"Florence."

The low rumble of Mr. Henry's voice was like the buzz of bees in slow-motion. Panic shot through me. I fumbled with the basket and stood up quickly.

Mr. Henry hovered over me, leaning on a cane. He stared, like he was waiting for me to say something. He was probably just waiting for a hello, but all I could think about was the bees.

"Mr. Henry, I know about your wife. I mean, I'm sorry about her. Marjorie." Her name caught in my throat. I had to swallow before I continued. "I want you to know that I'm moving away." I wanted to add a thanks-to-you comment, but I knew deep down it really wasn't because of the rent increase. Nothing unraveled completely with one big yank; it happened slower, tug by tug. "I don't need the bees for me, but for Candice. She'd be the best bee ambassador ever. That's what you want, right? More research for multiple sclerosis? Candice could do that if she wins at the festival with the bee beard talent."

Mr. Henry looked down at his cup of punch. He was quiet so long my hands started to feel sticky around the basket handle.

He cleared his throat and took a long sip of punch.

"Marjorie was diagnosed right after we were married. She went almost ten years without a single symptom. Then there were days she couldn't get out of bed because of pain and other days she could go biking without a problem. Until she got an infection." He paused and shook his head. "When she first had to start using the wheelchair I read up on apitherapy. You know what that is?"

"Bee venom."

Mr. Henry nodded. "It's honey, venom, all of it. I've been working for years to try to find a cure. About near gave up even keeping them bees when I lost so many last year." He stared down at his punch. "Marjorie would want those bees to still be helping others."

I nodded, because I didn't know what to say. Mr. Henry had said so many things, more things about himself than he'd said the entire summer.

"So, we have a deal?" Mr. Henry asked.

"A deal?"

"Yes, you gonna use my bees and help Candice win this competition, or not?"

I'd been thinking so much about Marjorie, I hadn't even realized he was offering us the bees. I nodded and reached out to shake his hand. "Thank you, Mr. Henry. You won't be sorry."

•   •   •

The punch wasn't pink or orange. It was a weird combination of both. Kind of like a sunset. Fran would have had something to say about the color dye and high-fructose corn syrup used to make it sweet. But it didn't matter. Punch was one of those things that you didn't really drink because you liked it or because you were thirsty, you drank it for something to do.

I scooped out two clear plastic cups of the orange-pink mixture and walked toward Candice. She was at the edge of the crowd, hovering close to her mom and Mrs. Thorton.

"Hey," I said, holding out the punch the same way you'd dangle a steak to a lion, praying that it was enough to keep them from eating you whole. Candice squinted at the cup, but took it. "We got the bees back."

"What? How?"

"Mr. Henry. He agreed. And Candice, I want you to take the entire prize. I don't need the money anymore."

The front of Candice's dress was covered in silver sequins that reflected the orange glow of the punch. "Your mom got the job, didn't she?"

I opened my mouth a few times to try to explain or pretend it wasn't true. I wasn't really sure which, because thoughts of both ran through my mind.

Candice sipped her punch. "I'm really sorry for being so mean all those times."

I sipped my punch too, because I didn't know how to tell her I was actually going to miss her. It was also because something inside of me tightened. That part of me that had been mean back to her, telling myself it was because she was mean to me first. I swallowed a few more sips of punch.

"I'm sorry too," I said. "I haven't always been the nicest to you, either. I just kind of got used to us not liking each other."

"Are you really moving?" Candice wiped her hand on the skirt part of her dress.

I shrugged. "Probably."

Probably.

Most likely.

Definitely.

Mom wouldn't give up the job of a lifetime. And maybe I was okay with that.

"I'm going to miss you." Candice grabbed me, squeezing me into a tight hug. I hugged back, leaving all the weirdness between us no space to stay.

Chapter Twenty-Nine

Random Bee Fact #77:
Twenty thousand bees followed a woman's car for two days because the queen was unknowingly trapped in the trunk.

The year I'd first been in the Honey Festival, it had rained. Not just rained, but poured buckets during the parade. People lined the streets anyway, holding plastic bags and umbrellas over their heads. I sat in the backseat of my Gramps's old-fashioned blue car. Of all the cars he'd restored it was my favorite and Mom had chosen my dress to match the paint color exactly. Only, because of the rain, I had to sit inside of the car instead of on the hood. Mom made me scoot from window to window and wave even though I don't think anyone could see me. Gramps and Mom had to take turns hand-cranking the windshield wipers of the 1950s Buick the entire stretch of Main Street and down Broadway, where the crowds ended. By the time we were to go onstage for the talent, the rain had stopped and you could see the puddles turn to steam in the humid heat that followed.

Since the ball, Candice and I'd practiced with the bees twice more. Her speech was finished and we'd timed it all out perfectly with the bee beard, and passed our projection video to Mrs. Thorton.

Candice and I spent our last morning at Mr. Henry's finalizing our plan to get the bees and the frame to the festival. Fran was still on board with helping Candice and me keep the entire act a secret. She jumped in to skim over Mr. Henry's questions about getting Dad to help out.

"Oh, Mr. Henry, I'll help you get things where they need to be." Fran busied Mr. Henry with the details while Candice shuffled through her speech a few more times.

He'd been keeping a close eye on the weather all week. We needed the temperatures to be in the not-too-hot, not-too-cool range and hoped it didn't rain.

Actually, there was a lot more than the weather we had to worry about. I wanted Candice to win. I didn't want to get stung and panic onstage or have Mom and Dad freak out when they saw the bee beard.

225

Saturday morning of the festival dawned bright and so clear, the blue of the sky glowed to an almost turquoise.

Fran burst into my room just as I rolled over to enjoy five more minutes of being perfectly cocooned in my bed.

"Flor, come on. We've got to get you ready before Mr. Henry shows up with the car."

Fran helped tape the dark plum dress I'd picked out with Mom around the boatneck collar and the cap sleeves. She was a master at hiding the tape. She's a knitter by nature—patient and particular. I crocheted because I was the exact opposite. I needed to be able to make mistakes, but in a way that was easy to work around. Fran thought we should tape the dress now since the talent show came right after the parade, and she might not have enough time then.

She even managed to get my hair just right once again. It was very me, but still dressy. Loose curls tamed my usual mass of tangled frizz and she pinned it all back out of my face. Fancy, but practical for the bee beard. Once my dress, hair, and makeup were done, Fran shoved a few more things into my clutch. "Look, if you need help with your makeup or hair, just ask me for help, or if you can't find me ask Candice."

A makeup emergency. Puh-leeze.

The parade didn't officially start until two in the afternoon, but Mrs. Thorton wanted all of us to be at the festival by noon. Around eleven, Mr. Henry pulled into our driveway and Candice's dad followed a few minutes later. Candice's dress was a light blue that made her hair and eyes shine like honey.

Candice gushed over my dress and how I'd paired it with the fingerless gloves I'd crocheted. Being around her was like changing yarn colors. You can let go of one colored string and start using another color and pick up the first color again when you need it. Even if you hadn't been using it for a few rows, it was easy to pick it right back up. Maybe it was because we'd spent so much time together that being around her felt normal, or it could have been knowing I was moving that made it easier to pick up where we'd left off before we'd hated each other.

After our parents and Mr. Henry figured out how to attach our blankets and mat to the hood of the car where we'd be sitting during the parade, Candice and I rode to town with her dad. Mr. Henry had to park with the other parade cars, and we'd meet him later before the parade started. Candice tapped the note cards against her chin and hardly said a word the entire way there.

I tried to think of something to say, something that would let her know she didn't need to worry, that her speech was really good. But nothing that came to mind had that sticking weight of truth; it all felt as light and airy as a helium balloon.

As Candice and I climbed out of the backseat of her dad's car at the meeting point downtown, a breeze made its way through the festival, picking up all the fried-food smells.

The streets were blocked off so that booths of food and crafts filled all the parallel parking spaces and left the middle of the street for the crowds to walk. The stalls were mostly selling food, and some sold specialty honey or baked goods with honey as an ingredient.

We didn't get to walk around: Mrs. Thorton wanted us behind the stage area to go over last-minute lineups. Carissa was already there, dabbing her face with makeup and staring into a handheld mirror. Her dress was sparkly and cut deep down her back. It made me feel underdressed in a dress I'd thought was fancy.

A few of the younger girls were there with their moms next to them, holding bags of their talent costumes.

In third grade I hadn't been nervous. Maybe because I hadn't expected anything. This was different. My heart felt like each beat was two beats instead of one.

"Girls." Mrs. Thorton clapped her hands to get our attention. A teenage boy with a clipboard stood at her elbow. "Thanks for getting here on time. After the parade please come back here to change for the talent show. You'll be notified three acts before yours and then again when the act before yours stars. Be sure any props are close by and that your music or videos have been cued."

Clipboard Boy flipped through some pages and held it out to Mrs. Thorton as she called the order we were to perform. Candice and I were act seven.

Before I knew it, we were lining up for the parade.

I climbed onto the hood of Mr. Henry's yellow Buick. Fran fanned out my dress and helped Candice get situated next to me. It felt like third grade all over again, when we'd been in parades after the Honey Festival, squeezed next to each other, giggling. Then, it had all felt endless, but right at that moment it felt final.

The parade cars lined up in Brooke's neighborhood because her street led right into Main Street and it was away from the crowds. Since the booths were set up along a few streets of downtown, the parade circled the outside of the festival.

The first car was Mrs. Thorton's, with the other city council members in the back of a truck bed. They were all dressed in yellow and black and wore headbands with antennae attached. Then the mayor was behind them, with her husband and children in a fancy convertible. After that, we were in order of youngest to oldest contestants. At the last minute, Mrs. Thorton had passed out sashes with our years bedazzled across them. They were in yellow and black and totally clashed with pretty much everyone's dresses.

I pulled out Fran's clutch and rubbed Vaseline across my gums, passing the tiny jar to Candice to do the same. I'm no professional pageant queen, but Mom had done this to me in third grade and, believe it or not, smiling for hours nonstop not only hurts your cheeks, it sucks all the spit out of your mouth so your lips stuck to your gums.

The cars crawled down Main and Broadway slower than you could walk. So slow I could see each face watching and waving on the other side of the barricades. I'm not good at guessing numbers. Looking at the crowd and trying to figure out how many people were at the festival gave me the same blank brain I got when I stared at a huge jar of candy and had to make a guess how many pieces were inside.

"Do you think the crowds are any bigger than last year?" I asked Candice, trying to keep a smile plastered on my face.

"Hard to tell," she said through her smile. Her arm moved in the beauty-queen-wave elbow-elbow-wrist-wrist pattern Mrs. Thorton asked us to practice. She made it look so normal, like it's how she was all the time. Not me—I probably looked like a malfunctioning robot.

As we pulled in front of Dad's store my smile slipped on the Vaseline that coated my gums. "Oh. No." I managed to clench my jaw while smiling and still talk.

Candice let out a laugh, but quickly smiled and straightened her back to cover it up.

"Not funny," I said, trying to keep a smile on my face.

"Kinda is," she singsonged back to me.

The largest picture I'd ever seen of myself—or anyone aside from the news anchors on a billboard—was draped in front of Dad's store. It was me in my powder-blue ruffled dress from the Honey Festival in third grade. One of my front teeth had only grown in halfway and the banner was so huge, my half tooth was even more noticeable than when it'd been in the newspaper.

Under my photo are the words: GO, SIS!

Fran hadn't called me "Sis" since I begged her to stop at the beginning of fifth grade. Mom, Dad, and Gram jumped up and down in front of the store, cheering so loudly for me that people stared at them. Brooke was there too. Ben and Sam next to her with balloons and shouting my name. The only person missing was Fran. She told Mom and Dad she was going around the festival with her friends. I swallowed down as much spit as I could get in my dry-from-smiling-too-long mouth because I knew Fran was with the bees until it was time for the talent show.

I swear Mr. Henry drove slower just to drag out my embarrassment.

Chapter Thirty

Random Bee Fact #101:
A queen bee only rules for two to three years before the
hive feeds royal jelly to larvae to replace her.

The slow, calmness of the parade melted faster than the soft-serve honey ice cream I stared longingly at. Mrs. Thorton motioned us all over toward her. Candice and I waved good-bye to Mr. Henry and followed Mrs. Thorton to the backstage area that had been set up between the library and the Golden Lamb. The stage looked small, even though it was higher than my head as we walked past it.

Behind the stage was surprisingly louder than the crush of the streets. Contestants were everywhere and Mrs. Thorton's organizational skills, rules, and commands all seemed to be completely forgotten.

Some of the tape around the neck of my dress had come loose because of sweating. I patted it all down and Candice flipped through her speech cards a few times.

"We've got this," I told her.

Mr. Henry kept the bees as far away from the crowd as possible, and I could feel the tightness in my arm and shoulder muscles loosen up as Candice and I made our way toward them, leaving the string of voices and press of bodies behind us.

The cage sat on top of a trolley with wheels. Mr. Henry and Fran would roll it to the steps and carry it to the center of the stage when it was our turn.

Mr. Henry met us at the cage. "I fed them sugar water, and the queen has been separated from them since yesterday afternoon," Mr. Henry said, and rubbed his hands together. He'd told us all of this when we were finalizing things at his house, but the way he kept rubbing his hands together made me think he probably repeated himself when he was nervous. "The weather is looking good, but if the wind picks up or any clouds start setting in, we'll have to pull it."

I crossed my fingers and turned to Candice. "The weather will be good. Everything's going to be fine."

Candice nodded and sucked in a gulp of air like she could breathe in my words to make them true. No matter how many things hadn't gone as I expected them to this summer, this was the one thing I wanted to go right.

We double-checked the cotton in my ears and nose and the Vaseline on my face. Dulling the constant noise from the festival with the cotton only made the too-fast flutter of my heart beating louder inside my head.

Clipboard Boy ran up to us and said we were three acts from going on, and again that we were next. The minutes went by too quickly and then Mrs. Thorton announced, "Our next contestants are Candice Holloway and Florence Valandingham with their duet." She moved to the side offstage as Candice walked up to the microphone stand. "Thank you all for coming to the fiftieth Honey Festival." The crowd clapped and I helped Fran push the bee beard cage into place.

Mrs. Thorton whispered to the stagehands when she saw the cage. Mr. Henry stayed off to the side with the frame of bees in a cardboard box covered with a newspaper so they wouldn't fly away.

Before we could get interrupted, Candice started her speech and the video we'd made started. A single bee bumbled across the screen between the curtains of the stage. Fran practically pushed me onto the stool inside the cage before disappearing off to the side out of sight.

Everything happened in slow-motion. The already-muffled talking, screaming, and noise of the crowd became a dull throbbing in my head. I was glad for the stool and that I'd be sitting for the talent.

The lights from the stage turned the crowd of people in front of me into a blur. It wasn't even dark out, but the stage was lit up. Only the newspaper photographers in the front row were visible.

Candice continued the speech as Mr. Henry made his way onstage. "Honeydale, Ohio, has held the Honey Festival for fifty years. But honey is only possible if there are bees." On cue the screen filled up with more bees. "Bees are nature's biggest helper. They pollinate the crops we eat. They keep the orchards healthy. Thanks to bees, twenty billion dollars' worth of crops are pollinated annually. But they're disappearing." A large group of bees fly off the screen. "You might think it's not a big deal. After all, the shelves at our grocery stores are constantly stocked with honey. In fact, Americans eat more than two hundred and eighty pounds of honey every year. And because of bees, more than one billion jobs have been created. And if you want to continue eating fruits, vegetables, and nuts, we need to make sure we keep bees healthy and thriving. Bees may have stingers, and I'm sure almost all of us have been stung a time or two, but bees are not dangerous unless they feel threatened."

Candice paused. It was the best dramatic pause ever.

She flipped to the next card while Mr. Henry clasped the queen bee around my neck.

"Watch along and see just how gentle bees are. More than twelve thousand bees will attach themselves to Florence's face!"

Mr. Henry held the tray of bees, covered in newspaper, waiting for my nod. Everything went from slow and faraway to superspeed as I nodded.

The crowd gasped as the cluster of bees fell from the frame when Mr. Henry shook it. The bees scattered and bumped around for a few seconds. Several bounced off of my face, but a few settled long enough to discover the queen. Then they flew off to bring the others toward me.

Before long, the pull of most of the frame of bees hung around my neck, making the bottom half of my face feel asleep like my arm had been during the parade.

The bees huddled in a clump, warming the skin around my lips and near my ears. The little itchy legs had made their home on my face enough times, I could almost sense what the bees were feeling. As they clamored on my face trying to keep the queen protected, they moved quickly like always, but not hurried.

The crowd had been mostly quiet, but as the bees settled on my face and stayed around my chin and neck, cheers erupted. Flashes from cameras and phones sparked at random. The bees tightened around my face and I gave the slightest nod to Mr. Henry. He warned me they could get grumpy if things got too noisy.

He brought the cardboard box and newspaper into the cage, closing the door behind him.

"And now Florence will return the bees back to their frame," Candice said into the microphone.

The bees squirmed and pushed against one another like bumper cars. I jumped hard and fast, letting the bees fall in a carpet onto the frame. More cheers erupted and Mr. Henry covered the frame with newspaper and nodded for me to step out of the cage.

I walked over to join Candice for a bow. Mrs. Thorton came up the steps and stomped across the stage, grabbing the microphone from Candice, her face as purple as my dress. "Thank you, girls. That was quite a surprise." She raised her eyebrows and gave us a look before introducing the next act. Candice linked her arm through mine and we both bowed. My entire body hummed with the warmth and buzz of the bees even after I'd shaken them off of me. Then I caught sight of my mom. Right in front of the stage, next to a guy with a big camera.

She didn't look happy.

We scrambled off as a little girl in a gymnastics leotard

took her place onstage. Mr. Henry and Fran had already rolled the bee cage down the ramp.

"I think my parents might literally kill me," Candice said, saying exactly what I'd just been thinking.

"I don't think they'll kill you. I'm the one who was covered in bees. Did you see my mom's face? She looked like she was going to throw up. I haven't seen anything that green since Fran made kale hummus."

"Did she really make kale hummus?"

"You've been eating her experiments all summer. What do you think?" I couldn't make up half the recipes Fran created even if I had an encyclopedia of food in front of me and picked stuff at random.

Cheers rang out as another performance finished. Mrs. Thorton's voice came through the speakers announcing the next act.

Music blared and Mrs. Thorton made her way down the steps, her clipboard in front of her like a battering ram. Candice and I shrank into each other.

When she reached us, her mouth was a tiny dot. She breathed in though her nose, making the buttonholes of her blazer stretch until they couldn't stretch any more.

"I'm very surprised at you two. You pulled quite the stunt out there. I could have you both disqualified for not getting that approved first. That was not piano-playing out there, Miss Holloway, nor recorder, Miss Valanding-ham. Not only was that a dangerous trick to attempt, I could hardly finish my job up there, I was so flustered."

"You can disqualify me, Mrs. Thorton," I said. "My part was the dangerous one. Candice only gave a great speech."

Mrs. Thorton opened her mouth like she could keep yelling at us until the fireworks started, but a guy with a headset walked up to her.

"Sally, the next act starts in ten seconds." He turned to us. "That was the coolest thing ever."

Mrs. Thorton shooed him away, then gave Candice and me a look through squinted eyes that made my feet stick to the ground. At the worst possible moment.

My parents and Candice's parents were walking right toward us.

Chapter Thirty-One

Random Bee Fact #34: In order to protect the honey supply during the winter months, worker bees kick out the useless drones (because their job is done).

Mom and Dad and Mr. and Mrs. Holloway stood in front of Candice and me, Gram and Fran behind them. Fran flashed us a huge smile and two thumbs up, but the parents didn't look so excited. Even Gram looked upset.

"What were you thinking," Mom asked, her voice loud, "having bees on your face?"

"Candice," Mrs. Holloway started. "To put Florence in that kind of danger and not even say anything . . ." She turned to Mom. "I'm so sorry, Mina. If I'd have known . . ." She shook her head.

"How could you two even come up with such an idea?" Mr. Holloway asked.

Candice and I exchanged looks, but neither of us could think of anything to say. I guess I knew my parents might freak out, but we hadn't thought about the time between our act and the end of the festival when they'd announce the winner and our parents would come backstage. We had hoped we'd be announced the winner and that they'd forget to be mad at us.

"I'd like to know why Mr. Henry was up there helping," Dad said.

"They were his bees," I said. It wasn't *really* an answer, because a lot more questions had been asked, but it was the only answer I wanted to give right then.

Heavy footsteps came from behind us.

"Would you like to explain yourself?" Dad asked.

Mr. Henry nodded slowly. "I understand you're upset."

"'Upset' is an understatement," Mom said.

"These girls were supposed to be helping you with yard work," Mrs. Holloway added.

Mr. Henry nodded again. "Yes, they were. After being around the bees a few times, they asked if I'd train them. They were never in any danger."

"You couldn't know that for sure." Mom stepped forward. "You didn't think to call us and check that it was okay with us? What if one was allergic?"

"I'm sorry. I didn't—"

"Think?" Mom finished for him.

Dad put his hand on her arm. "Mina. Mr. Henry, I think what we're all trying to understand is—"

"You know what?" I said. "This isn't Mr. Henry's fault. It was my idea."

"*Our* idea," Candice said. "We both wanted to win and we knew we had to do something big."

"Don't blame Mr. Henry; we told him you were okay with it." I stared at the ground littered with wrappers, blue feathers, and sparkles and pretended to feel 100 percent guilty, when really I only felt about 20 percent, and that was because Mr. Henry was getting blamed by our parents and we'd lied to him about having their permission.

Dad shook his head. "Well, it certainly was a show-stopper."

Mr. Holloway chucked and nodded.

Mom gaped. "You can't possibly—"

Dad put his hand on Mom's arm. She didn't flinch away like she'd been doing lately. Ever since Gram arrived, Dad had been less angry about letting the store go and Mom had been more relaxed. "But it was also thoughtless, Flor. Don't you ever do something like that again without talking to us about it first."

"Yes, you girls had good intentions, but you really should have had our permission first," Mrs. Holloway said.

"I really meant no harm," Mr. Henry said.

Dad turned to Mr. Henry. "Thank you for keeping them safe."

More cheers erupted and Mrs. Thorton asked the crowd to come back later for the crowing of the queen.

"Well, I think we should just . . ." Mrs. Holloway motioned for Candice to follow her, and Mr. Holloway moved closer to the stage. Mr. Henry nodded and apologized again as he made his way over to the bees still covered in newspaper inside the cage.

Once we were standing there, just me, Mom, Dad, Fran, and Gram, all the adrenaline that had filled me a few seconds before rushed out. I felt tired and empty.

Mom was the first to wrap her arms around me. Then Dad. Then Fran. Then Gram held on to us all.

An hour later, after finding Brooke and sharing corn on the cob, slathered in honey butter, and smoky honey barbeque ribs, Candice and I stood with the other contestants in a wide U shape on the stage with Mrs. Thorton in the front, holding up an envelope and waving it in the air. The microphone screeched as she walked too far to the right.

"This year's festival has been so successful thanks to

the hard work of all the busy bees on this stage with me."
Cheers and clapping filled the air. She smiled widely as her
eyes scanned the row of us, but her eyes squinted when she
got to Candice and me.

"We've had quite a hive this year, but there can only be
one queen." She paused and let quiet settle over the crowd.
"The fiftieth Queen Bee is . . ." The envelope made a *clicky-
pop* as she opened it. "Candice Holloway, for her informa-
tive speech and creative display of bee knowledge!"

Candice turned to me and squeezed my arms with her
hands as she bounced up and down. I pushed her forward
to where Mrs. Thorton was standing with the crown.
Attendants at the edges of the stage filled her arms with
flowers once the crown was placed on her head.

Somehow we ended up backstage and Brooke ran to
us, jumping up and down and hugging Candice and me
at the same time.

Mom and Dad congratulated Candice and pulled me
aside.

"The fireworks don't start for a while," Dad said. "Go
and have fun with your friends. We'll meet you in front
of the store at nine." He passed me some money and they
walked off, holding hands—something I hadn't seen them
do in a long time.

Brooke grabbed my arm and linked elbows with Candice. "This calls for some honey ice cream."

I turned back to ask Fran if she wanted to join us, but she waved me off. "I'm going to catch up with my friends—they're waiting at Aunt Bee's."

"You guys get the honey ice cream. I don't even like that stuff," Candice said.

Brooke shoved her playfully. "How can you say that? We're at the Honey Festival in Honeydale, Ohio!"

Our laughter mixed with the sounds and smells of the festival. I inhaled the stale deep-fried air and closed my eyes, trying to wrap every little thing about right then in mental Bubble Wrap to keep it all safe forever in my memory.

Everything I thought I loved and hated about Honeydale surrounded me: my family, Brooke, Candice, Mr. Henry, Dad's store, the festival. None of it was the same as it had been at the beginning of summer, but all of it was exactly how I didn't know it should be.

Even moving to New Jersey had become one of those things I never imagined would be good, and maybe it wasn't in the way honey was good, but it was in the way Fran's cauliflower rice was healthy-for-you good. Mom got the job of her dreams. Fran had already called around and found a food pantry at which to volunteer. Dad was excited to "hang up his sales hat and put on his lawyer suit." And me, well, a new school might not be so bad. They did have a state-of-the art computer lab.

I think if an apple hit me on the head right then, not even the laws of gravity could drag me down.